Dance To The Music

Also by the same author

Aunt Maud's Windmill (Marshall Pickering)
Beyond Healing (Hodder & Stoughton)
The Broken Stone (Marshall Pickering)
The Fire Brand (Marshall Pickering)

Dance To The Music

a sequel to *The Broken Stone*

Jennifer Rees-Larcombe

Marshall Pickering

Pickering and Inglis
Marshall Pickering
3 Beggarwood Lane, Basingstoke, Hants RG23 7LP, UK

First published in 1986 by Pickering and Inglis Ltd
Part of the Marshall Pickering Holdings Group
A subsidiary of the Zondervan Corporation

British Library CIP Data

Larcombe, Jennifer Rees
   Dance to the music.
I.   Title
823'.9145 [J]   PZ7

ISBN 0-7208-0690-9

Text set in Plantin by Brian Robinson, North Marston, Bucks
Printed in Great Britain by Anchor Brendon Ltd, Tiptree, Essex.

The author gratefully acknowledges the enormous help of Tim Bentley of the rock band Quaizar and Richard Belcham in the preparation of this manuscript.

Contents

1: Manda   9
2: Problem Parents   18
3. Total Contrasts   26
4. The Anarchists   34
5. Acceptance   44
6. The First Gig   51
7. Surprises   59
8. A Step Backwards   65
9. A Transformation   73
10. Reactions   80
11. Manda Rises to the Occasion   86
12. Zac's Surprise   94
13. Jesus, Where Are You?   102
14. Tragedy   109
15. Troubles for Zac   116
16. Aftermath   122
17. A New Zac   133
18. An Uncertain Future   141
19. The Passion Play   150
20. More Trouble   158
21. A Terrifying Climax   169
22. God's Victory   179
Epilogue   183

Chapter One

Manda

Ants! Black ants scurrying from every direction and converging on a giant ant heap. I looked down on them from the high windows of the fifth year common room. One thousand two hundred ants in black blazers. It was the fourth of September – the first day of term and a new school year. Yesterday Gravely Comprehensive had been an empty deserted shell, today it was pulsating with life.

I turned from the window and surveyed the room behind me. The noise was unbelievable. Girls greeted one another with wild shrieks of enthusiasm and everyone competed with Radio One as they tried to swap holiday reminiscences that no one else wanted to hear. Funny how girls can change so much in only six weeks. Some had worked so hard on their sun tans that they were almost unrecognisable, they all seemed to be either much fatter or very much thinner, and their hair! The straight ones had gone frizzy and the curly ones straight. Why do girls do that to themselves?

That was the first day our year had a common room of our own, but already you could see the groups forming up – marking their territories. But where did I fit in? All the years that I had been at Gravely I had always known just who I was and where I was going, but during that summer holiday rather odd things had started to happen to me. I can only describe them as mental flashes of lightning, but they were profoundly disconcerting. You can go through life accepting yourself without a second thought and then suddenly you look at yourself from the outside, and you wonder 'who on earth am I really?'

The swots were already huddled round a table in the corner judging the merits of various teachers by last year's exam results. I suppose I was a swot really—I had determined to come out of Gravely with three A's at 'A' level, but I did not love work for its own sake as they did. It was just a means of getting me where I wanted to go, so I did not fit in with them. They bored me.

The sport freaks were scuffling round in their new lockers talking loudly about teams and match fixtures. I shuddered —how I hated the sporty lot!

The couples had naturally hogged all the sofas and were at it already. How can anyone be that passionate before nine in the morning? I did not fit in with them. 'Fat chance', I thought bitterly. No girl would be seen dead on a sofa with me. I could hardly describe myself as Mr Universe.

The music lot looked scruffier than ever. I have often wondered if they hired a specially trained fleet of moths to work on their uniforms during the holidays. I could well have been part of them because music is my life, but they never wanted to know me because I played the guitar and sang my own songs. The Gravely music department are so purist that any music that was written less than one hundred years ago simply does not exist for them.

Naturally the greatest volume of noise was coming from Zac's lot. They had formed themselves into a group right from the first year, and because they had always been anti-work, anti-sport and anti-teachers they were known as the Anarchists. Zac sat in the middle of his bobbing crowd of admirers, nonchalantly lolling in his chair with his feet on another. I noted with envy that he was better looking than ever. People were talking to him from every direction, but he never attempted to answer them. Yet he attracted people to him as surely as if he had swallowed a powerful magnet. Something always niggled in my memory when I looked at Zac. He reminded me of someone – someone I knew well, but who was it? I forced my eyes away from Zac, angry with myself because I admired him. I had always disapproved of him and his Anarchists and all the aggro they caused in school, so why did they secretly fascinate me?

My eyes travelled on round the room. The odd lot were hanging together as usual. They did not really fit in with any group as they draped themselves pathetically round the walls. I did not want to land up with them, so I finished my visual journey rather suddenly and focused at last on us. This is where I had always fitted before, but that day I realised I just did not belong any more. The Christian Union at Gravely has always been a safe little world within a larger one. We knew each other well, we had grown up together, most of us went to the same church, but because my father happened to be the minister of that church, they all tended to keep me at arm's length, and it's lonely sitting on a pedestal – especially if you know that secretly you are not really worthy to sit there at all. I was never just David Martin, I was David Martin the minister's son. So I had to act the part, smile at the right people, say the right things, react in the right way; but as I stood there that morning, I knew I was a hypocrite and I despised myself.

'Who do you think will lead the CU now Dan has left?' asked Dominic, and I noted with quiet satisfaction that his acne was worse than ever.

'You could David,' said Pam, with one of her infuriating giggles. I had wanted to lead the Christian Union ever since my first day at Gravely. After all, I had always planned to become a minister myself one day like my father, but *I* would have an even bigger church than his, and people would travel the *world* to hear *me* preach. I turned my back on the CU crowd, their cheerful faces irritated me. As I looked out of the window, I realised that I had always been like someone walking down a straight concrete road towards a definite destination. But now I felt as if I had been sucked into a squelchy sinking bog with no incentive for trying to climb out again.

Suddenly, something happened in the room behind me. It was rather as if a guillotine had fallen and cut off all the sound. Conversations were left in mid sentence, giggles and squeals hung in the air as a stunned silence settled on the room. I swung round and there in the doorway stood Manda. The shock of seeing her again after six months was enough to hush anyone. Was it possible that any human being could change so much? I remembered how she had looked last September, a healthy, cheerful, uncomplicated girl. Even though she was in the year ahead of us, I had always secretly fancied her. Of course, that was only until she had been sucked under the spell of her evil friend Mary Jenkins, and when I say evil, I mean *evil*. Mary's life was full of bitter, spiteful, vindictive hatred and she had bullied Manda into helping her set up a blackmail and protection racket last autumn that brought havoc to Gravely, causing some teachers and pupils real and lasting harm. Around Christmas time, Gravely had started to call Mary a witch and when one of the teachers had died after a row with her, a witch hunt had tried to stone her behind the new Sports Hall. Mr Atkins, our Headmaster, called them old fashioned and superstitious, but when Mary had been discovered peddling drugs round the school, he had asked her to leave.

It is strange how fast minds can work in a few seconds of time. I could feel people all round me recalling those terrible events of last winter. As we all looked at Manda's

12

little shrivelled body standing in the doorway, I could feel the hostility mounting against her as they remembered her connection with Mary. But that was not fair. I knew something that most of them did not know. Manda had changed. In the middle of all the tragedy and chaos she was helping to cause, she had suddenly realised what a hopeless mess her life was in, and she had handed it over to God and become a Christian.

Gravely had never had a chance to recognise that change, because a dreadful thing had happened. Only a few weeks after Manda had become a Christian, she and Mary had been out late one night, when a drunk had driven a car right at them. Manda had flung herself at Mary, pushing her out of the way, but the car had hit her instead and she had spent the last six months at Stoke Mandeville Hospital mending a broken back.

The unfriendly silence in the room was horrible, and I saw Manda's drawn white face begin to twist. Was she going to burst into tears? She must have felt horribly isolated standing there alone facing a room full of hostile strangers. All her year had either left or gone into the sixth year block and it must be hard to have to go down into the year below to do all the exams she had missed.

Suddenly I remembered who I was – the minister's son. I had been trained since before I even went to Sunday School to 'make new-comers-feel-welcome'. So I rushed across the room and took her hand. It felt like the brittle claw of a tiny bird as I pumped it up and down. The tension in the room was relieved and the noise began to flow back like a stream that has been temporarily dammed.

'When did you get home from hospital?' I asked as I drew her across the room towards our corner.

'Two days ago,' she gasped with a slight echo of her old smile. She clutched a walking stick in her right hand and seemed to have a job remembering how to make her legs work. She looked like a robot with faulty wiring.

'How's Dan?' I asked to mask my embarrassment. Her strained face lit up when I mentioned her boyfriend's name.

'He's off to art college in two weeks,' she replied and as I looked down at her face, suddenly pink and animated, something twisted inside my chest. Would any girl ever look like that when my name was mentioned?

Of course the Christian Union knew all about Manda. We had prayed for her at church and here at school. Dan had given us up-to-date progress reports each week.

'You're a miracle really, aren't you?' I said as I steered her round the Anarchists. 'No one thought you would walk again did they?'

'Well I hate wheelchairs so much that I don't care how odd I look when I walk. Anything is better than spending the rest of my life in one.' I admired her determination, but I could see how much the ordeal of that walk across the common room had cost her by her sigh of relief when the welcome of the CU engulfed her.

'Whose class are you in?' I asked as I slid her walking stick under her chair.

'Miss Carmichael's,' she replied.

'Bad luck,' laughed Dominic, 'she's a raving atheist.'

'I know,' grinned Manda, 'and I'm not looking forward to it much.'

'She's a very interesting person,' I put in, springing to the defence of the most attractive woman I knew. Since I had started my flashes of doubt, I had found myself really looking forward to being in her class and having a chance to talk to her. If someone as intelligent and attractive as she was had definitely decided there was no God, then maybe she could be right.

The shrill ringing of the electric bell cut across all the

activity of the common room, and everyone began to disperse in all directions for registration.

'You go on, David,' said Manda, 'I'm so slow, I'll only hold you up.' But I wanted to shield her from all the embarrassing stares and hostile glances she would meet on the way, so I said, 'There's no rush, we're only down the end of the corridor,' and picking up her bag I slung it over my shoulder.

'I'd almost forgotten how huge Gravely is,' she said ruefully. 'I only came in today to get my timetable. I have to go to physiotherapy every day and I still get tired and have to rest a lot, so I'll only be coming in part-time.' As I looked at her struggling along that corridor I really did not feel she was fit to be back at school at all. She was powered by nothing but guts. When I asked her what subjects she was doing, I realised we would not be seeing much of each other, and I caught myself feeling that was rather a pity.

However, the human whirlwind that is Miss Carmichael soon banished Manda from my thoughts. 'She really is a magnificent woman,' I thought as she harangued us from the front of our classroom that morning.

'This is the most important year of your lives,' she declared. 'The results you get in the exams this year will decide what 'A' levels you take, and they will decree what you do in life. Today you must decide whether you are going to grow up, work hard and make something of yourselves or just flop back and drift.' Was it my imagination or was she looking rather pointedly across the room at Zac?

Just at that very minute I felt one of my flashes coming. I fought it hard, but it came on relentlessly. It was as if a fierce light was illuminating my life, forcing me to see what it was really like. Part of my role as the minister's son was to be 'good at school work'. A bad mark reflected on Dad's good name, or so I had always thought. I had spent years sweating away at my homework and doing extra back-ground reading, but now as the flash took its course, I wondered why I had bothered. If the Bomb was going to destroy us all and end our civilisation what was the point of working anyway? Why not just enjoy the short span of life still left to us?

That flash did rather rob the morning of all purpose, and I was so bored I was thankful to get back into the common room to eat my packed lunch. But just as I dashed in through the door I bumped violently into Manda. Her walking stick shot into the air and she landed on the floor with her heavy sling bag of books on top of her. As I picked her up I felt acutely embarrassed to see tears running down her thin white face.

'I'm terribly sorry,' I said. 'Let me carry your bag. Where are you going?'

'Don't worry,' she said, forcing her face into a smile. 'Dad's waiting in the car outside. I'm just flaked out, it's a bit of a strain coming back to school; I'd rather manage on my own.' But I practically had to carry her downstairs in spite of her fierce independence.

'David,' she said suddenly, as a herd of noisy third years surged past us, 'David, thanks for talking to me this morning. If you hadn't come across that common room when you did, I think I'd have run away for ever.'

'All part of the service,' I said, putting on my minister's son act. I could do it well after years of practice, but inside my head I could feel another flash coming on. As I looked down at Manda's shattered face I felt like screaming *why?*

I could understand that accident happening if she had still been destroying people's lives, and playing round with witchcraft, but she had changed – told God she was sorry, and I had always been taught to believe that when we do that, He forgives and forgets. Yet not a month later, God

16

allowed her life to be smashed up. How could He let that happen to her? Could there really be a God of love if He allowed suffering?

Outwardly I was still the minister's son as I helped Manda into her father's car, and waved them away, but inside I felt shaken to the core of my soul.

Chapter Two

Problem Parents

When I got home from school that evening, I felt as if I had literally been struggling in that muddy bog all day – I was shattered. I dropped my bag on to the floor with a dispirited thud and flopped on to my bed. What was I going to do about myself? These flashes were getting right out of control. Once I would have prayed. I had always asked God what to do when anything bothered me. But if there wasn't a God, then there did not seem much point in talking into the air. I laughed ruefully, when I thought of how many people came from all over the country to discuss their problems with my parents, yet I felt too embarrassed to talk to them myself. The only other people I could have gone to, were members of our church and the minister's son can't very well bounce up to someone and say, 'I don't believe in God any more.' It would let Dad down horribly, and anyway, he'd be bound to hear about it and feel hurt. Everyone told Dad everything. So I really might just as well go to him in the first place, but when? Getting Dad or Mum on their own in our house was no easy achievement.

The crescendo of noise and activity below me indicated that it must be supper time, and my heart sank. How I *hated* supper time in the Manse. Our house is a huge, grotesque, Victorian mistake, and I loathed every inch of it as I walked downstairs that evening. So many people always squashed into the kitchen to be with my mother that Dad had knocked the wall down into the dining room to make one huge 'living space', where Mum reigned like a queen bee surrounded by innumerable drones. But as I opened the kitchen door that September evening, the noise would have drowned the hum of fifty bee hives! The enormous old-fashioned kitchen table that filled almost half the room was still only just large enough to seat the five thousand who had come to be fed! Of course, I'd always known ever since I was tiny that because Dad was a minister we were not an ordinary family, and anyone who was in trouble or had nowhere else to live, would come and stay with us. Mum was always saying, 'How wonderful that God gave us a house with eight bedrooms.' Since the flashes had started, I had often wished He had only given us one with two, but I never quite dared to say so.

It was the noise at meal times that really got to me. Two particularly squawky babies were being shovelled with cereal by their chattering mums. One had run away from her husband because he battered her, and the other had never even had a husband in the first place. The piercing wails and screams told me that Kevin was here for supper again. He sat hunched in his wheelchair while his mother too stuffed cereal into his mouth. It went in at one corner and dribbled out of the other. Ugh! I could not look. It was bad enough with the babies, but Kevin was my age. I supposed it was not really surprising that Kevin's Mum had been an alcoholic before she started to spend so much time in our house. She was on her own with Kevin and if you only had that to look at all day, you might as well turn to drink.

George was chuntering on as usual. George is a tramp; he likes being one. He sleeps in empty houses or on park benches, but Mum insisted on giving him one good meal a day. The penalty for being late for supper at the Manse was having to sit in the only empty seat, which was always next to George. You had to keep your nose out of action by breathing through your mouth – the smell was terrible. He had no teeth and his jaw wagged up and down when he ate. It had fascinated me as a child, but it was getting a bit much now, and so was his endless talking. He never stopped. No one ever listened, but still George carried on adding to the general cacophony.

I squeezed in between Pam and John, thankful to avoid the penalty seat for once. It was already occupied by a rather dazed-looking stranger. Pam had been kicked out of her home by her father, and as I listened wearily to her incessant giggle, I really could not blame the man. John was all right; I rather liked him. He was living with us while trying to kick a heroin addiction and he was managing very well, but the drugs had done something horrid to his stomach and he belched frequently and with total abandon. It could be jolly funny if it happened in church or during grace, but when you're trying to eat your supper it doesn't really aid the digestion.

'Had a good day, Davy?' shouted Mum across the table. She did not wait for a reply, but continued her intense conversation with the visitor who sat between her and George. She obviously had what Mum called 'deep problems' which meant Mum had to keep her eyes fixed on her, saying 'Oh dear!' and 'How sad,' while she dolloped stew and mashed potatoes on to plates without looking at what she was doing. Suddenly I wished I could tell her I had 'deep problems' too so she would listen to me like that.

Dad's place at the end of the table was empty because it was Bible Study night. People came from fifty miles away to his weekly lectures which were recorded, and the cassettes were sent all over the world. He spent so long preparing them he never came out of his study at all on Thursdays.

As I gulped down my food, trying not to look at Kevin, smell George or murder Pam, I imagined myself standing up and shouting, 'I don't believe in God any more!' What would they all do, that is, if they even heard me? Mum would probably say, 'Don't disturb your Dad, Davy, have you forgotten it's Bible Study night?'

I watched her, fascinated, across the table. The 'deep problems' seemed to be coming to a dramatic climax.

'Poor dear!' said Mum and she served a whole ladle full of milk jelly right into John's tea cup. I pushed my chair back from the table. I'd had enough!

'Don't you want any pudding dear?' said Mum without taking her eyes off the visitor's woebegone face. I looked at the jelly cream turning to grease on top of the cold tea and said, 'No thanks,' very firmly.

'Well don't go yet, you're on wash-up tonight, with Pam.'

'I've got too much homework,' I growled, knowing perfectly well that she would not argue with me in public; our image of a happy, united family was far too important to her.

As I crossed the hall it did just occur to me that I might pop in and talk to Dad right then, but years of being told 'never to disturb Dad when he's preparing', held me back. Why couldn't I have an ordinary family with a father who came home at six after earning lots of money, and a Mum who had nothing to do all day but cook lovely expensive things like steak or pork chops? Ordinary fathers tinkered with the car or the lawn mower, and could always be talked to whenever the need arose. Why did mine have to be kept in cotton wool behind closed doors?

As I climbed the stairs I had to pass the long mirror that hangs at the top. I wondered if the spot on my nose had got any bigger that day, it felt enormous. I looked at my reflection as if I had never seen it before. I must have been in the front row when noses were given out; mine's gigantic. But why didn't I get a chin to match; the one I was lumbered with recedes so rapidly I look just like a woodpecker; and the spots are just the last straw. I had never cared much about my appearance before (after all, ministers don't need to be handsome), and I must have spent hours in front of this mirror working on my preaching techniques, practising for the time when people would flock to hear me, read my books and ask me to straighten out their lives. But suddenly I realised I had no future. If there was no God, what was the point of a career in the church. It certainly didn't bring in much money – but what else could I do? Inside my public image, I was such a non-person I was bored to tears just living with myself.

I climbed on up the next flight of stairs to my attic bedroom. I loved it up here; it was my own private world; I could be myself; I did not have to act any more. I picked up my guitar which had long been my escape route, and began to tune it. All my life I had thought my parents were perfect, but why did they live as they did? Was Dad a minister just because he liked having power over people, and did Mum fill the house with lame dogs to boost her own self-esteem? Was the church work they did just a substitute for other people's bingo, golf or bridge?

I began to play my latest song. I don't mind saying I'm pretty good with the guitar. I had led the worship at Gravely CU and the church youth group for a couple of years and Dad often asked me to sing one of my own songs in church. Everyone would smile lovingly at me and whisper, 'What a ministry of music the Lord has given him.' "

I cringe now as I think of it. But this latest song was different. It was accompanied by angry, aggressive chords and I knew full well Dad would certainly not want these words sung in church.

The volume of noise in the house was going down. The babies bawled themselves to sleep, George had gone off down the road still talking, and the visitor had driven away in her shiny BMW. If I had a gorgeous car like that I wouldn't sit about grizzling, and I wondered if Dad ever minded having to drive round Fleetbridge in the terrible old banger the church had 'kindly' given him.

I watched from my window as Dad and Mum walked over to the church and felt as if a cold bucketful of misery had been flung over me. It suddenly became incredibly important to talk to them; it was like a physical ache. I needed their reassurance. It is no fun being sixteen; you are not a child or a man; you hang suspended in nothing. I longed for them to convince me there really was a God. If I could not rely on my parents or myself, how was I going to cope if God wasn't there either? Suppose the Bomb really did go off? If heaven was only imaginary, where do we go when we die? Black nothingness? And what was life *for* anyway?

With all these cheerful thoughts to keep me company, the evening passed quite quickly, and soon they were all home again. The two mums and Pam went chattering and giggling upstairs followed by John belching loudly. Now was my chance. Mum and Dad would be alone. She was warming Dad some milk on the Aga when I walked into the strangely empty kitchen. Dad was slumped in the armchair beside the stove looking completely drained. He always looked like that at the end of Bible Study night – as if he'd just had a severe haemorrhage.

'You're still up, Davy,' said Mum. 'You *must* have had a load of homework.'

'I need to talk to you.' I began awkwardly. I had practised this speech so many times already, but now I felt like an actor who has forgotten his lines.

'I'll make you a hot chocolate,' said Mum, bustling off to the fridge for more milk.

The 'phone rang.

'Hang on a minute love,' said Mum drawing the milk off the heat, 'I'll just answer that.'

As I listened to her voice in the hall, I realised by her tone that she would probably be hours. Suddenly I saw myself in this very room, probably aged about seven, playing snakes and ladders with her. I was winning, then the 'phone rang. She was reading me a story a few years earlier and I was sitting on her knee. Just as we reached the exciting part – the 'phone rang. I'd cut my knee and she was wiping the blood away and talking about finding a nice big plaster, when – the 'phone rang.

'The story of my life,' I thought bitterly. Dad had his hand over his eyes as if they hurt, he didn't even seem to remember I was there.

'Dad, I really do need to talk to you,' I said feeling mean because he looked so tired.

'Fire away then,' said Dad without moving his hand, his voice sounded mechanical and as if it was coming from a great distance. He is such a small, frail looking man while Mum seems twice his size; even her glasses are enormous. I always wish I had taken after her and not Dad. I pulled a chair up in front of him and firmly planted myself in it.

'It's just that I . . .' The doorbell rang.

'Pop and see who that is Davy,' said Dad without moving.

On the doorstep stood one of the church youth group. Her face was swollen with crying and her hair stuck out of her head like a moth-eaten doll.

'I can't stand my parents any longer,' she sobbed, 'please let me see Mr Martin.'

No one had ever been turned away from the door of the

24

Manse, so I stood aside and then followed her back into the kitchen.

'I've seen it happen before, so I wasn't surprised. Energy seemed to pour into Dad. It always did when he had to do what he called 'a job for God'. His exhaustion left him, his colour returned and as he sprang out of his chair I could not help thinking he looked ten years younger.

'Rosey, my dear,' he said. 'Whatever is it? Come into my study and maybe David will make you a coffee.'

He was giving her all his attention, and he could not even bother to address me directly. As the door shut behind them and I was alone, I felt I could not stand my parents any longer either. Viciously, I rammed the plug into the back end of the kettle and out loud into the empty kitchen I said, 'I don't care whether there's a God or not, one thing's for sure, I'm never having anything more to do with Him.'

Chapter Three

Total Contrasts

I was halfway across to the church hall the following
evening before I realised what I was doing. Friday night
meant Youth Group, and that had been the high spot of my
week for three years now.

'But you can't go to church or Youth Group if you and
God don't mix,' said a voice in my head, and I stopped,
startled in my tracks. 'I suppose I *can't* really go,' I thought,
putting my guitar down on the garden wall and leaning my
elbows on it. But if I cut all that out, what would my life
contain? It was not so much what we did on those Friday
nights, it was just being together that was fun, drinking
coke or coffee and then I'd reach for my guitar and we'd
sing. Two or three people might say what God had done for
them that week, and then we'd pray. Well it was more like
chatting to God really, telling Him about the things that
were on our minds. Of course, all that had been getting
increasingly difficult since the flashes had started earlier
that summer, but now it was going to be impossible. But
the Youth Group were my friends – they might irritate me
sometimes, but they were all I'd got, and if I said I wasn't
going to church any more, what would Mum and Dad say?
Serve them right! They didn't care about me. But all the
same I would be cutting myself off from them rather
suddenly wouldn't I? Yet I must climb down off that
pedestal. I couldn't go on pretending. I must grow up

whatever it cost. I picked up my guitar and turned back towards the Manse. But whatever was I going to do all evening? There wasn't any point in doing any homework, not if I'd decided not to bother about exams. Suddenly life did not have any structure – nothing and no one to button it on to. Once again, I stopped halfway up the garden path as I remembered what Mum had said as I had gone out of the door only a few minutes before.

'Look after Manda, won't you Davy? She's coming to the Youth Group tonight, and her mother told me today she's very anxious about it. She never used to be shy, but since she came out of hospital she's got terribly self-conscious.'

'So would anyone be self-conscious,' I had thought, 'if they walked like a puppet on strings.' But I had promised to look after her. So with an enormous feeling of relief I turned back towards the church hall again. If anyone saw me cannoning up and down our garden that evening, they must have thought I was a complete wally.

'I wonder if Manda ever had any flashes when she was in Stoke Mandeville,' I thought. 'Surely she couldn't go on believing in a God who let her down like that. I'll ask her tonight.' With this good excuse for going to Youth Group to wave in the face of my conscience, I walked on feeling much happier, and once I had decided to invent a sore throat so I would not need to sing I began to look forward to the evening ahead.

The church and hall had once matched the Manse in old-fashioned ugliness, but Dad's preaching had attracted such huge crowds that they had become far too small, and had been replaced by wonderful new buildings that were the envy of most Baptist churches in the country.

Everyone was there – except Manda. My eyes searched the crowded room in vain. There was Rosey, all smiles and sparkles – whatever Dad had said to her last night had

27

certainly cheered her up. John was in excellent belching form, and Pam's giggle was more penetrating than ever.

'My mum's buying me a sunray lamp to cure my acne,' said Dominic. 'You ought to get one David.'

'Fat chance,' I thought sourly. 'My parents can hardly afford to buy me a new pair of socks, let alone a poncey solarium.' But my evening was ruined, and Manda still had not come. I was just about to discover that my 'sore throat' needed to be taken home to bed, when suddenly there she was and I cursed myself for being such an idiot. I should have remembered. Manda didn't need me to look after her, she had Dan didn't she. But surely he didn't have to make quite such a fuss – just because he was her boyfriend it didn't mean he owned her. He helped her through the door, got her a chair and a coffee and then stood over her for all the world as if he had created her himself.

He'd changed a lot had Dan. Once he had been very way out in his clothes and hair cuts, but now he almost looked like a Conservative candidate. Why do all Christians conform to the same mould?

'You do look cross tonight, David,' complained Pam with a giggle.

'I am,' I replied, 'so shove off!' The minister's son had never talked like that before and she gave me a startled look. Why was I feeling so irritated with Dan, when I had always liked him so much? He had been my complete idol at Gravely. Suddenly I saw him heading in my direction.

'That wall'll fall down if you don't keep propping it up,' he laughed. 'Have you got your guitar?'

'Yes, but I've got a sore throat,' I lied. 'I can't sing tonight.'

'I know, Mike told me.' (Mike's our Youth Pastor.) 'But I wondered if you'd lend it to Manda. She's written a song, and I've persuaded her to sing it.'

'I didn't know she could play.' I did not mean it to sound as rude as it did.

'She taught herself in hospital – she had plenty of time to practise there.' I handed it over and he fussed at the piano, tuning it for her. Everyone clustered round, and when Dan had settled Manda on a stool he called for some hush.

'Manda wanted me to tell you all how much your cards and letters meant to her in hospital, but most of all she wanted to thank you for all your prayers. She feels that's what got her through, and brought her back here *without* a wheelchair!' 'Why couldn't she make her own speeches?' I thought sourly. 'She made up a song while she was away,' finished Dan 'and now she's going to sing it for us.'

Everyone clapped loudly and put on 'encouraging' faces. This was probably going to be rather bad, but we were determined not to show it. But we need not have worried. As soon as she began to play, an almost liquid silence descended on us. She only played simple chords – the kind of thing I'd been doing years before and her voice was small, but there was a plaintive sweetness about it that compelled you to listen. You could sense that the music was coming right from her soul. The song was all about how she had felt when she woke up in a hospital bed and found her legs wouldn't move any more.

> *I thought you'd deserted me Lord*
> *hurting – frightened – alone.*
> *But there in my fear you came to me, Lord*
> *More real than ever before.*

So she *had* doubted God, but He had become even more real to her – how? I really needed to know.

When the song was finished it seemed to hang in the air. No one clapped – they did not even move; and several people were crying.

'Play it again, Manda,' whispered Mike. I think they must have made her go through it about four times, and soon they were all singing with her. Lots of people prayed for her then, asking that she would have enough strength to cope with school work and all the physiotherapy; and honestly, I hoped God heard them, because as she sat there clutching my guitar she looked so frail, I felt she might fall over if someone happened to sneeze.

Everyone crowded round her at the end asking her all kinds of questions – most of which Dan answered for her. Why couldn't he stop smothering her? I was so disgusted I longed to walk out, but Manda still had my guitar so I had to hang about, while my irritation mounted.

'Thanks, David.' The voice behind me made me jump. Manda must have pushed her way right through her cloud of admirers, and every part of my being seemed to tingle as she handed me back my guitar. I'd always thought her hair was red before, but I realised then that it was every shade from newly hatched conkers to a royal gold, and I adored the way it curled around her face.

'I liked the song,' I said awkwardly.

'You didn't look as if you did,' she laughed.

'Well I feel bad tonight with my sore throat,' I said lamely. 'But I really did like it very much. I could teach you a few more chords and some different techniques sometime if you like.'

'I hoped you'd say that,' she blushed. 'Thanks, I'd love that. Dan's told your Dad about my song, and he's asked me to sing it in church sometime, but really I could never do that on my own. Would you sing it with me?'

The thought of giving her guitar lessons was delightful, but how could I sing in church again now?

'Manda,' I began, clearing my throat loudly. 'When you felt God had deserted you . . . how did you . . . when did you . . . ?' *Blast!* There was Dan, barging his way over towards us.

'I've promised to get her home by ten,' he said. 'Come on love, I've brought the car right up to the door.'

BLAST! BLAST! BLAST! Was *no one* ever going to have the time to listen to me?

I did not go straight home. I just could not face it, so I gave my guitar to John, and went for a walk. I think I must have been heading for the common, but I never got there. Old Fleetbridge had once been a sleepy old market town snoozing beside the common and it has never lost its character, even now a thriving new town has grown up around it. I was walking down the old High Street with its tea shops and antique businesses when I heard music that was strangely out of context in that living history book. Turning down a side alley, I stopped outside the seedy exterior of Hallen Hall. For years it had been the home of a youth club that had the worst reputation in Fleetbridge.

'They've got some kind of a gig there tonight,' I thought as the music from the open doors and windows hit all my senses at once. Flocks of motorbikes were tethered outside, but it was the van that really invited my attention. It was painted all over with psychedelic colours, with the words ZACKARY AND THE ANARCHISTS picked out in luminous green. I knew Zac was into drama – he and his lot were always putting on sketches, and I'd heard they were in demand all over the district – but I had no idea they had music as well.

It was a warm evening, so I could see in through the open door. The place was full of what we called punks in those days. Black leather jackets, gleaming with metal studs; hair sticking up stiffly from partly shaved heads and dyed every colour of the rainbow. They jumped and leapt about to the music that boomed from the stage above their heads while the disco lights flashed eerily through the haze of cigarette smoke. It was such an alien world to the minister's son, I could have been standing on Mars.

Their sound was not very good, even I knew that. In fact they were only held together by the drummer – he was magnificent. I knew Trev at school, but there he was a very different person. He hated being one of the few black kids at Gravely, and he put on a constant act as a smoke screen. In those days robotics were right in, and Trev moved round school in a series of detached jerks which drove the teachers insane. But behind those drums I saw the real Trev. He must have had at least eight arms, each one gleaming with sweat in the spotlights, while his long woolly hair shook and vibrated with every flick of his head. I was bewitched.

Suddenly guitars, keyboard and drums were cleared hastily to the side of the stage and the musicians became actors as if by a flick of a switch. The audience booed and stamped. They wanted the music to continue, but as Zac's sketch rolled into action, the noise in the hall died away and soon you could have heard a knuckle crack.

Zac was certainly no punk. You could not describe him as a skinhead or a casual either. He was Zac and no one else, but he put on a punk's wig for that sketch, and leathers too. He had to appear before a bench of magistrates on a charge of 'being alive'. I had often seen him act at school, so I already realised just how brilliant he was. The whole thing was hilariously funny, but under the slapstick it said some very cutting things about our society. Why should people be judged by what they looked like? The audience shouted and cheered their appreciation as they identified with Zac in the dock. The Anarchists' music might sound amateur, but their drama was polished and professional. I found myself really needing to know how the sketch would work out in the end, but suddenly a huge figure with multi-coloured hair barred my view of the stage.

'If you're not stayin' and payin', why don't you get out?' he said rather nastily. I would willingly have paid, but as usual was skint. so I walked off down the alley struggling to collect my thoughts. Even with only that brief glimpse, I had recognised that Zac was a genius. The lazy, drawling, switched-off act that he put on at Gravely was every bit as much of a front as my minister's son performance.

Chapter Four

The Anarchists

Someone sneezed. Startled, I looked round the empty room, but there was no one there. It was Monday lunch hour, and I had taken cover in the music block. I was quite lucky really to be at school at all. I had used my imaginary sore throat to get me out of going to church the previous day, but Mum had threatened to take me to see Doctor Davison, so I'd had to recover with a rapidity that bordered on a miracle. I was hiding now because I could not think of an excuse for not going to the Christian Union meeting, so I had simply disappeared.

As I had walked down the corridor in the music department, I could hear that all the practice cubicles were full of discordant sounds, so I had slid into one of the three classrooms where I knew no one would bother me. To my joy, I saw one of the school guitars had been left out on the teacher's table and I grabbed it. They are pretty horrible specimens, but I fiddled about with the strings until it was just about bearable, then I began to work on my new song. It sounded even angrier than usual that day, and I managed to add a couple of quite pithy new verses. It was all about growing up in a polluted world with only the Bomb as a future.

Why did you have to be born
Into a world you've spoilt?

that was the hook that kept recurring. I was rather pleased with it – and then someone sneezed.

I looked round the room in great embarrassment. I hate being overheard when I'm exposing my soul, but no one seemed to be there. Could someone be in the big cupboard at the back of the room? As I walked over to see, I nearly fell over Zac stretched out full length on the carpet with his head on his bag of books. He looked as if he was asleep.

'What are you doing here?' I demanded.

'Just nursing a hangover,' he replied without opening his eyes. 'One can get rather sick of people sometimes.' I suppose you might if you had as many buzzing round you as Zac always did.

'That song – who wrote it?' He spoke so softly I almost didn't hear him. 'You did, didn't you?' Slowly he sat up and looked at me with his lazy dark eyes. 'It's very good you know.' I was surprised and deeply flattered.

'Thanks,' I croaked. 'The guitar's terrible, but I've got a better one at home.'

'I'd like to hear you on an electric guitar with a really good amplifier and a mike for your voice.'

'Fat chance!' I snorted.

'I've got all that round at my place,' said Zac casually. 'Why not drop round tonight and try them?' I'd heard his Dad was wealthy, but this was ridiculous.

'What time shall I come?' I asked rather breathlessly. 'When do you eat?'

'We don't,' said Zac shortly. 'Come about seven, you know where I live?' I nodded. Everyone knew. With his father's great Rolls Royce parked outside no one could miss it.

I found my heart beating rather fast as I crunched up the sweep of gravel in front of Zac's house that evening. It was an old Elizabethan farmhouse nestling in a fold of the common, and it seemed very imposing to the little church mouse who nervously approached the front door. I knew Zac's father was some kind of foreigner. He looked like an oil sheik as he drove round the town in his Rolls. What would his wife be like – was she foreign as well?

The carved oak front door was opened, after a very long delay, by a dazzlingly attractive woman in a filmy pink negligee, edged with floaty white fur. I was so surprised I stepped backwards and nearly fell down the step.

'I've come to see Zac,' I stammered, feeling miserably conscious of my nose, not to mention the spot on the side of it!

'You should have gone round the back,' she said irritably flicking back her long blonde hair. 'He's in the stable.'

I felt rather confused as I walked round the outside of the house. Zac was a lot of things, but you could hardly describe him as horsy.

Behind the house, the old farmyard had been beautifully paved and dotted with tubs of exotic flowers and brightly coloured umbrellas stuck in white wrought iron tables. Through a stone archway I could see a swimming pool, but there was not a horse in sight. The farm buildings had been rebuilt and adapted to provide garages, but one large barn seemed to have a stable door, and as the top half was open I peered in. The lofty room was candlelit, and the smell of joss sticks was pungent.

'Come in,' said a lazy voice from the gloom. 'I thought you'd never get here.'

The room was huge and as my eyes became accustomed to the dark, I looked around in amazement. This certainly must be the Anarchists' home base. There was the set of drums I had seen Trev playing, with the keyboard and guitars beside it. In one corner was a bar like a miniature pub, and in another was a huge mirror surrounded by light bulbs like they have in the dressing rooms of theatres. All kinds of costumes and theatrical props littered the place, and there in the middle, sat Zac with his feet on a small table on which stood a bottle of vodka.

'Over there,' he said, nodding to the guitars. 'It's the red one you want.'

I froze. The whole atmosphere of this place inhibited me. The good little minister's son inside me was positively quaking with fright.

'Come on,' said Zac, taking his feet off the table and stubbing out his cigarette. He switched on the amplifier, plugged in the lead guitar, and humiliated me by lowering the mike.

'All right,' he said at last, 'off you go.'

'I'll make such a noise,' I protested. 'What about your mother?'

'My mother!' sneered Zac. 'That's not my mother, that's just Dad's latest. He *calls* them secretaries. Pagh! But if it makes you happier . . . ,' and he shut the top half of the stable door. 'Now we're completely soundproofed, so you can take the lid off.'

At first I was so nervous my voice sounded thin and squeaky and my fingers fumbled with the strange instrument. But gradually I began to relax, and as Zac fiddled around at the mixer desk, balancing my voice and the guitar, I could hear how good it was beginning to sound.

As I watched him, I realised Zac had changed. The cool, detached image was gone. Suddenly he was alert — interested — professional. He was a born showman and a great producer. As I sang, he walked round the stable listening from different vantage spots, adjusting the balance and nodding encouragement. I could feel him building my self-confidence and drawing the best out of me.

'It's good, Dave,' he said at last. 'It's very good. The others are coming round in a minute. We'll have a jamming session – they'll pick it up in no time. Have some vodka.' Dad always said that he counsels so many people with drink problems that he would never have alcohol in the house, so I had never tasted any – we even have grape juice at communion.

'No thanks,' I said, 'I've just had my tea.' I could have bitten my tongue out, it sounded so silly. Zac smiled sardonically.

'I forgot your dad's a vicar,' he said, and suddenly I hated him. He had everything I wanted – good looks, money and charm, so he felt he could mock me and put me down.

'I could use a beer,' I said coolly, like people do on the telly.

'Help yourself,' he grinned, waving towards the bar. 'There should be loads of cans in the fridge.' I did not much care for the taste, but it made me feel less like a baby.

Zac poured himself out an astonishingly large glass of vodka and said, 'I've been looking for someone like you for a very long time, Dave.' I swallowed my beer the wrong way, and spluttered with sheer surprise. 'We're getting loads of gigs now, because people like our drama, but they do want music as well. Trev's always been a magic drummer, and the others are improving all the time, but we do need a really good lead guitar and vocal. Steve thinks *he* can do it of course, but he's only a rhythm player, and his voice lets us all down. How would you feel about joining us? You've got everything that it takes and a good bit more.'

'What about Steve?' I said nervously. 'Won't he mind?'

'Everyone round here does just as I tell them,' said Zac quietly and fetched me another can of beer from the fridge.

I can see myself now, standing there clutching it in both hands, not realising at that moment I was suspended

38

between two worlds, belonging to neither. But I began to grow up the moment I said, 'All right then, I'll come in with you.' And as I pulled the metal tag from the top of the can, I experienced the same fizz of relief that the beer must have felt.

The first two to arrive were Trev and Joe. They crawled in through the bottom half of the stable door and eyed me with hostility. I knew Joe had not been with the Anarchists for very long. He and his identical twin brother had arrived at Gravely at the same time as the rest of us. Both their parents were university professors, and Joe's twin was a mathematical genius. But poor Joe was not an academic, and he was crippled by an appalling stammer. He struggled desperately for the first couple of years to live up to his brainy family, but when he was fourteen he freaked out completely. He did not look remotely like his twin any more. Martin still had his short back and sides and immaculate white collar and tie, but Joe had let his hair grow long as a floor mop and his clothes would have revolted a tramp. He played the synthesizer about as badly as he did everything else, but he could act quite well so long as he did not have to say anything.

Monkey did not come through the door – that would have been too easy. He swung himself through a small window behind the stage, and then proceeded to stand on his head. He was always doing that at school. He said it helped feed his brain cells, and he certainly had plenty of those. I found it most disconcerting to be glared at from upside down, and I realised that Zac must have told them all he was going to ask me to join them. The CU and the Anarchists had never exactly hit it off, and they must have thought I was an enemy infiltrator.

'Tess and Michelle aren't coming,' said Monkey. 'They're voting with their feet,' he added, looking at me pointedly.

'I'm not crying,' said Zac sourly, but he looked annoyed all the same.

The candles sent gigantic shadows prancing up the walls, and in the silence the tension mounted – we were waiting for Steve. The beer in my insides began to swirl and lurch about as I remembered that Steve was a karate brown belt, and he was always boasting that he could kill a man with a chop from one of his gigantic hands. I'd been terrified of him ever since he had been the bully of the infant school we had both attended. He must have been at least twice the size of me, and if he wanted to be the lead singer, perhaps I had better disappear while I still had a head.

Zac, however, seemed completely unaware of the suspense as he sat smoking his Turkish cigarettes. Surely he would never make Steve accept me, so I began to sidle towards freedom. But my escape route was barred by the massive Alsatian dog that had slunk in through the stable door.

'Here's Steve now,' remarked Trev as the dog, who was always Steve's shadow advanced towards me showing his yellow teeth, while the hair rose along his skinny spine. His name was Devil and it suited him.

'What's he doin' shoving his great conk in 'ere?' demanded Steve as he banged the stable door shut behind him.

'He's our new lead,' said Zac, putting his feet back on the table. Steve helped himself liberally to vodka and they eyed each other over the rim of their glasses, like two wolves vying for the supremacy of the pack.

'Give your song a spin, Dave,' said Zac softly without taking his eyes from Steve's face. I doubted if anyone ever had a more hostile audience.

'We don't want him!' roared Steve when I had fumbled my way to the end, and he brought his huge fist crashing down on the table making the glasses rattle. Zac said nothing as he blew a smoke ring, and watched it float away into the shadowy rafters high above.

'I'm not saying we don't need a lead singer,' continued Steve, sounding slightly disconcerted by Zac's silence, 'but why *him*! He's nothing but a little holy, holy, holy choirboy. Just look at him!' Devil snarled, as if to emphasise the point, and as they both stood glaring at each other it was hard to say which one looked the most unpleasant. If I had been Zac, I would have been terrified, but he is about the coolest cucumber I've ever encountered.

'His appearance we can change, man,' he said soothingly. 'It's the sound that counts. Now why don't you all go and see if you can get the hang of this song, because it would be ace for Saturday night.'

Grumbling and muttering they picked up their instruments and the dog took his place at Steve's feet eyeing me with disfavour. We ran through the song several times while they got the feel of it, but it sounded terrible. I could tell it was all wrong, but I did not know what we could do to improve it. Zac did not seem to be even listening. He sat with his back to us, blowing smoke rings and sipping his vodka. I was just about to throw down the guitar and leap for the stable door and my old safe life, when he took his legs from the table and sprang up. Suddenly he was his other self again.

'Now then,' he said, 'let's get at it. This number depends on mounting tension, and that's up to you Trev. You're going to start with an intro on the bass drums, very slow and dismal, then Joe comes in with the spooky church organ effect, which brings David in. But we'll keep the pulse right down at the start and gradually build up as the anger mounts until we get to the final verse, then you can really let it go Trev. Same goes for you David. You go from a low state of depression at the beginning, right up to wild rage. We could even finish with you screaming, "Why did you have me born?" But you can't just stand there like something out of Madame Tussaud's. By that last verse, you've got to be stamping and leaping round the stage. Here, give me your guitar, I'll show you.'

'It's all very well doing all that when you're not singing,' I protested as I watched him in consternation, 'but I'd never have the breath.'

'Look, it's never enough just to sing a song. You must think of the visual effect – express the words with your face and your whole body. Move man, move!' I panicked. I was right out of my depth.

'Have another beer,' said Zac going to the fridge, 'that'll loosen you. Now Joe and Steve, you'll do a backing vocal with David in the hook each time, so will the girls. Good close harmony, and each time you do it, it's going to get angrier.

It was hard to believe that Zac couldn't play a single instrument – he played people instead. He had an uncanny knack of knowing just what each of us should be doing, and bit by bit that song began to take shape. I lost count of how many beers Zac encouraged me to drink, and they were on their third bottle of vodka when we took a break to listen to ourselves. Zac's recording equipment was so good, I thought we sounded terrific, but it may only have been the beer.

My memories of the rest of the evening are rather fuzzy for obvious reasons, but I do remember Steve saying, 'You'll have to do something about yourself before Saturday, Concorde,' as he looked me over contemptuously. 'You could hardly call yourself a sex idol could you!'

I might have felt hurt if it was not for the beer, but I remember laughing helplessly and wondering if I was beginning to sound like Pam.

'We won't get back until Sunday morning,' sneered Trev. 'What's Daddy going to say if you miss church?' Vaguely I remembered that Trev had attended our Sunday school until he had joined the Anarchists.

'Look,' I said, with as much dignity as all that beer would allow, 'I'm my own person. I can do what I like with my own life.'

But not it seemed with my nose, because as I staggered home through the dark streets that night, I must have walked smack into a lamppost and broke the wretched thing – the nose I mean, not the lamppost.

Chapter Five

Acceptance

The Manse beds down incredibly early. Mum and Dad get up about five to pray, so they do seem to flake out about ten. When I still was not home by midnight, they panicked. The good little minister's son had never been late home in his life. I had told them I was going round to a friend's house, so they started ringing half the CU and Youth Group – waking snoring fathers and irate mums. It caused quite a stir I can tell you. At one o'clock they even rang the police, and it had to be them who found me, didn't it! Sitting under a lamppost, with blood all over my face, singing my new song at the top of my voice.

I don't remember a thing about it myself; not until we reached the hospital and I found myself sitting on a hard chair listening to someone behind a curtain having their stomach pumped out. They must have taken an overdose, and I've never heard anything so horrible. The police and nurses were not at all sympathetic about my accident, and my nose was beginning to hurt like mad even through the effects of the alcohol.

Suddenly Mum and Dad were hurrying through the swing doors, and I was so glad to see them, I was sick all over the floor. They must have smelt the beer and they both drew back in horror.

'They told us you'd had an accident,' said Dad, 'but you look as if you were in a fight.'

'I walked into a lamppost because I was drunk,' I snapped. I wanted to shock them, but I had to wait for their reaction while a nurse mopped up the mess I'd made on the floor, tutting and making 'serves you right' noises as she did so.

I really hoped Mum and Dad would start getting on at me. We had never really had a family row. They had always expected me to be good, and I always had been, but I was beginning to think that all the things I needed to say to them could only be said in the heat of anger. But once again I was thwarted. It is impossible to have a fight with two people when you are convinced that they are both praying for you inside their heads.

'Well it's obviously broken,' said the sleepy looking doctor when he finished his ghastly job behind those curtains, and he eyed my nose as if it revolted him as much as it had always disgusted me. 'I'll get a nurse to pack it.'

While we waited for this horrifying form of torture, Mum said, 'I suppose you wanted to see what it felt like – being drunk I mean.' She was desperately trying to find an excuse – an honourable way of repairing the image she had of me, as her good little Christian son.

'I was thirsty, and they didn't have any coke,' I growled, and as a nurse wheeled the dressings trolley towards us, the conversation ended on a painful note.

Two days later I walked into the fifth year common room, to the accompaniment of loud hoots and derisive laughter. I knew I looked a complete fool. Both eyes were navy blue and almost completely closed, while a huge dressing covered my nose, almost obliterating my whole face.

'We heard you had a spot of bovver getting home,' sneered Steve, 'but this is ridiculous!'

'If a few beers do that to him, Heaven help him when he

45

starts on shorts,' added Monkey. Zac was lolling in his usual chair and he beckoned me over to him, rather like a king condescending to give an audience. As the ranks of the Anarchists closed round me, I was conscious of the startled faces of the Christian Union as they watched me from the far side of the room.

'Well, that settles it,' said Steve with satisfaction, 'we can't take him on Saturday looking like that.'

Zac surveyed me at length through half closed eyes. 'When does all that plaster come off?' he asked at last.

'Not for a week at least,' I answered miserably.

'Well, it's coming off on Saturday,' declared Zac firmly. 'I can see his whole face painted white, with purple lips and eyebrows. If he wears those mirror glasses we've got in the props they would reflect the disco lights and distract attention from his face as well as covering his eyes.'

'But what's he going to wear, for goodness sake?' said Steve scornfully. 'One of those choirboy's frilly collars? And just look at his hair!'

I had always rather liked my hair, and felt it was my best feature – should I say my only feature!

'What do you think, Michelle?' said Zac addressing a girl who was leaning affectionately over his chair. 'Michelle is in charge of our make-up,' he added by way of explanation as she began to pull at my hair with professional fingers.

'It's not a bad length on top,' was her final verdict. 'With a good jell it should punk up quite well.'

'Bright pink, would be best,' said Zac, 'draw the eyes away from his face.'

This was getting too much. They were discussing me as if I was a pedigree dog at Crufts.

'I can't have pink hair!' I protested as I imagined myself sitting down to Sunday lunch in the Manse, or worse still arriving at Gravely on Monday morning.

'It comes out with a good shampoo,' said Michelle flatly.

Suddenly her place at the right hand of the throne was taken by Tess, who pushed the others away as if they had been a litter of annoying kittens. She must surely be the most electrifying, attractive girl in Fleetbridge. She had never even deigned to speak to me before, but I had often dreamed of her doing so. Most boys in the year competed for her favours, and even the male teachers went bendy at the knees when she looked in their direction. In my dreams, she looked *up* at me in admiration, not *down* at me in scorn. 'If *you* look that bad,' she said mockingly, 'how much of the lamppost did you leave behind?' 'She's like a lion,' I thought as her image quivered before my eyes. Her auburn hair stuck straight up from her head like a tangled mane and she had a way of showing her white teeth and biting the air in your direction, which I found disturbingly attractive. Her figure tried to burst itself out of her school uniform, and I reckoned other girls must hate her on sight.

'He's one of us now,' said Zac firmly, 'and with any luck he'll teach you to sing.'

Tess looked down at him with a seductive snap of her white teeth. He was the only male on whom her charms were entirely wasted, which of course made him her number one quarry.

'Pity he's such a little runt,' said Steve, putting his arm possessively round Tess's shoulders.

'We'll certainly have to get him looking more masculine,' agreed Zac. 'Trev,' he called authoritatively, 'that leather jacket and boots you got up Petticoat Lane last Sunday — David's wearing them on Saturday.'

Trev froze in the middle of a display of robotics he was performing on a nearby table, and he gazed at Zac in horror.

'Like rotten compost he's not,' he spluttered. 'They'd

47

have cost me over a hundred quid if I hadn't nicked them.'

Zac did not even bother to argue, he just assumed his word was law. 'You got some tight jeans to wear with them David?' he asked. Last year's jeans had become very tight indeed since Mum had accidentally boiled them with the nappies, so I nodded.

'Speckle them with bleach,' said Steve. 'I *suppose* you do know how to.' Suddenly I'd had enough of their sarcasm. Even a runt with a huge nose and two black eyes had his pride. They could keep their silly group. However frustrated I might get with the CU at least they did not insult me.

Zac is a born leader, and has a sixth sense to warn him when he is pushing someone too far. Just as I was about to elbow my way out of their company for ever, he uncurled himself from his chair and putting an arm through mine, led me away towards Miss Carmichael's room.

'I've been listening to those recordings,' he purred, 'and they're great Davo, really ace! Your appearance we can change, but your sound! We like it just the way it is.' I liked being called Davo – anything is better than Concorde.

'If you'd written that song specially for Saturday, you couldn't have done anything better. It fits my sketch like a glove.' As he talked, I could feel my ruffled feathers falling sleekly back into place, and I was even able to ask, 'What is it actually that we're doing on Saturday?'

'Well,' smiled Zac, 'there's this multibillionaire who's a client of my Dad's, and it's his daughter's eighteenth birthday. She's having about 200 guests and some of them are really influential show biz people. She's on a Ban the Bomb kick at present, so I've done the sketch specially, and your song fits it like magic.

We were still early for our geography lesson, so he sat down on my desk with his feet on the chair. We could hear

48

Miss Carmichael's voice booming in the distance, sounding as if she was addressing the Communist Party Conference on the floor below. As people flooded into the room and took their places round us, Zac went on talking to me as though I had been the most important person in all the world, and suddenly I discovered that I liked him. Yes, I liked him a lot.

'Do you write all the plays yourself?' I asked.

'Write them! No way. Plays can't be written down and taught to performing budgies and then rehearsed to a state of boredom. I get an idea and then we all 'feel' it – let it grow until we become part of it. It's a joint effort. Spontaneity – that's what we go for. They're all very good – except Tess, and she looks so good it doesn't really matter what she says or does!'

Manda had come into the room behind us, and suddenly I realised she was perched on the desk next to mine.

'You do a lot of political sketches, don't you?' she asked, sounding genuinely interested. 'What colour's your politics?' Zac chuckled, 'We're anarchists, aren't we?' He replied softly, but the crooked little smile he gave her was a strangely gentle one.

'I thought anarchists used guns and bombs,' she laughed.

'We use words for weapons,' he said. 'We make people think.'

'Do you get many bookings?'

'More all the time,' he replied. 'Now we've managed to convince the local landlords we're not under age, we get gigs in all the pubs and clubs. But we get a lot of parties and private do's as well.'

It sounded an incredibly glamorous life to me, but Miss Carmichael's voice could be heard vibrating up the corridor, and our conversation ended abruptly.

'Come round to the stable tonight Davo,' ordered Zac as

he swung himself from my desk. 'We're having a full run through for Saturday.'

He had won. I was under his heel for ever. The only thing that spoilt my happiness was the anxious look in Manda's eyes.

Chapter Six

The First Gig

We were so tightly packed into that van on Saturday evening, we felt like an unborn litter of piglets. The van was dangerously overloaded, but with Big Jim driving it like a Ferrari at Brands Hatch, it was positively lethal. He was the only one of the Anarchists who was not at Gravely. Zac had introduced him to me as 'our road manager' but he was for Zac what Devil was to Steve. I believed that he would cheerfully have died for Zac, but I was to discover later that I was wrong. Steve, Devil and Zac sat in the front with him, while the rest of us wrapped ourselves round the gear in the back. Because I was the newest, and most despised member of the Anarchists, I was squashed between the roof and the PA speakers, with Simon's feet in my face.

'Give Davo plenty of sound tonight, Simon,' called Zac over his shoulder. 'Steve's still drowning him.' Simon was the boffin of the Gravely physics department – a whizz kid with all things electrical. He looked after all the equipment for the group, working at the sound mixing desk and controlling the lighting panel. He grunted vaguely, and blinked at me like an owl through his thick glasses. I was feeling distinctly fragile after the afternoon I had just spent in the stable at the mercy of Michelle. My face was so caked with white make-up, it could not have smiled if it had wanted to, and I hadn't dared look at the reflection of my punked pink hair in case I died of shock. But most of all, I was miserably conscious of the extraordinary shape of my nose when we took off the plaster.

'Oh dear!' Zac had said when he had looked me over anxiously. 'We're not going to get away with this unless we put out a rumour that you're some kind of a flyweight boxing champion.'

As the van hurtled towards London, I looked down from my elevated discomfort and surveyed the other Anarchists. I'd had plenty of time to observe them during rehearsals that week, and I could not help thinking what an odd lot they were. Laughter had been completely banned – perhaps they had never learnt the art in the first place. I could not help comparing them with the Youth Group, and the fun we had always had when we squashed like this into Mike's van to go to a Christian concert or to lead the worship in another church. Tess and Michelle were constantly bitching at each other, while Steve kept up a barrage of snide remarks about my appearance and Trev glared at me balefully. He could not forgive me for wearing his new jacket and boots.

Monkey was a strange character, I thought as I tried to shift my position without causing the worst to happen to my incredibly tight jeans. On stage he was undoubtedly the comic of the outfit. He is Jewish, and used all the wit and humour of his race to reduce people to helpless laughter. His crinkled, rubbery face gave him his nickname, and he could use it to brilliant advantage. But off stage, he withdrew into a private world of lonely bitterness that no one could penetrate. He had to take a good deal of aggro at school because his parents were orthodox, and would not allow him into school assembly. But he also received a lot of flak at home because he associated with what his parents called Goys, and would not be confined to their Jewish community. I could see his life was not easy for Monkey. Perhaps he was no more sure of his real identity than I was.

My arm and leg were beginning to fizz with pins and needles, while a mixture of diesel fumes and lack of oxygen were making me feel travel sick.

'Oh, God,' I prayed earnestly, 'don't let it happen in here.' Then I realised with a dull thud that there was no point in praying if there was no God, and even if there was, He certainly wouldn't be interested in my prayers any more. It had not been easy at lunch time that day telling Mum and Dad I was going out, and would not be back until the next day.

'But where are you going?' asked Mum blankly, as she ladled out the mince and boiled rice. If I had said I was going to form part of a cabaret act for a party that would last all night, they might well have collapsed with apoplexy. So I had to paint them a vague picture of a musical evening in a stately home, at which I had been asked to sing. Pam and John sat with their mouths open as I managed to convey an impression of a gold embossed music room, plenty of harps and lutes and the odd harpsichord chucked in for good measure. I think I did it quite well, and I finished by saying, 'I'll try not to be too late for church.' That was my master stroke, but I felt a heel when I remembered that I did not intend to go to church that Sunday, or indeed, ever again. I don't think Dad and Mum were taken in for one minute – they both looked deeply miserable, and I had a sudden mad longing for them to lock me in my bedroom, and forbid me to go out. Of course, they would never do such a thing, and even if they did, I would probably climb straight out of the window. But all the same as we gyrated along in the van, I profoundly wished I was back at home.

When Big Jim brought the van to a skidding standstill, virtually catapulting us all through the windscreen, I realised my abstract impression of the stately home had been prophetically accurate. As we crawled stiffly out of the van, the regency elegance of the enormous house over-powered us all.

'No way is this my scene, man,' said Trev, going into one of his robotic routines to cover his embarrassment, and when a real live butler opened the ornate front door at the top of a sweeping flight of steps, Monkey immediately stood on his head. But Zac seemed perfectly at home in these imposing surroundings, and as he strode up the steps I could not help thinking how gorgeous he looked. He wore the kind of clothes I have always longed to possess, and the crisp yellow and white of his outfit showed off his dark skin and hair to perfection.

'Good evening Harper,' he said pleasantly, 'can we leave our van here while we unload?'

'Certainly Sir,' beamed the butler, 'but Miss Carolyn would like to see you first. Come this way, please.'

'Miss Carolyn would like to see you,' mimicked Monkey, doing a brilliant impersonation of the butler as we all followed him into the marble hall.

I had been to lots of places like this one before, but never without having to pay at the door. Mum has a passion for stately homes and ruins every holiday by dragging me and Dad round as many as she can spot on the map. But some-thing was wrong with this one. I realised as we followed Harper through a chain of rooms, that he was the only genuine thing in the house. All the 'antiques' were too perfect to be really old, and the colours of the carpets and curtains were all too bright. Everything was what my old Gran would have called 'common' and I began to have a distinct impression that the money, which had bought everything we saw, had not been earned honestly.

'Zaccy, darling!' screamed a shrill voice as we were

ushered into what looked like a great ballroom. 'I've been positively dying for you to come.' Her voice sounded as artificial as everything else in this house, and I assumed this must be the birthday girl. She flung herself ecstatically into Zac's arms as if they had been going out with each other for years. It was quite a surprise when he told me later they had only met once before. Tess eyed her murderously, but 'Miss Carolyn' was such a scruff I could not see why Tess was worried!

'The disco band are going to muck along in here,' continued our hostess, 'and I thought you'd be better in the hall, so people can sit all the way up the stairs to watch the drama. We're going to have a simply marvellous squeeze. Fortunately, Mummy and Daddy have popped off to Switzerland for the weekend to take cover, so we won't have any "inherbishes".' She did not sound as if she had a plum in her mouth, I reckoned it must have been a large melon.

'Come and have some drinkies,' she said drawing us into a full-scale bar. 'Your people can unpack the stuff.' 'Our people' were Big Jim and Simon, and they did not look at all pleased. Trev's boots felt at least four sizes too large on me and with the tight jeans as well, walking was somewhat hazardous.

'Come on Davo,' said Zac eyeing me critically. 'Get a few shorts down you quick, you look as sick as a church mouse before the Bishop arrives. Don't waste time on beer or you'll spend all night in the loo.'

'I'd better stick to coke,' I said, wanting to be sober enough to give my new song a good start in life. But Zac handed me a double whisky.

'You'll sing like a bird after three of these,' he said. 'I can't possibly act until I'm thoroughly legless.' Everyone else was downing them at lightning speed, and I could feel Steve's eyes on me—mocking. So I swallowed them like medicine and by the time the guests began to arrive, I felt magnificent.

I look back on that first night with the Anarchists and see it as a series of 'takes' from a horror film. We were given three slots during the evening, and the first was very near the beginning. 'Miss Carolyn' rounded up all her guests and squashed them into the hall.

'Darlings,' she lisped through my mike, 'here are the Anarchists. They really have something important to tell us about the world situation.'

We were supposed to kick off with my song, but Joe flipped so badly on the keyboard that we had a terrible job to get ourselves going. Of course, I had sung many times before to far bigger audiences, but they had always listened attentively to the lyrics. My songs had been a message from me to them, or rather God communicating through me. So I found it very unnerving when they continued to mill around talking loudly, and greeting their old friends with rapturous shrieks of recognition. We were no more to them than background music in a supermarket. I peered out at them from behind my dark glasses, trying to see what they were like. Most of them looked as if they had just been on a 300 miles CND march and hadn't bothered to wash or change before coming over. Then I caught sight of Zac gesticulating at me wildly, and I knew he wanted me to hop about and stamp with fury, but I dared not in case I burst my jeans, and the whisky was making me feel sick.

They did settle down a bit for Zac's sketch. It would have been most unsuitable at an ordinary party, but with this lot it went down like honey to a sore throat. The bombs had dropped and annihilated Britain. Seven survivors were left struggling to build a new life. It was brilliantly done, and Zac's acting genius made it tragically convincing. Monkey's wit and Trev's robotics prevented it from becoming too

56

heavy, and Tess's every appearance was greeted with loud whistles and hoots. The whole thing ended in thunderous applause. But after that the audience began to get bored and started drifting back into the ballroom, and the disco band clashed with us so horribly, we decided to concede them the victory.

By the time we did our second set, they had all had so much to drink they did not want to be told anything important about the world or anything else for that matter, and the two sketches that the drama group did were so incredibly crude I must have turned scarlet with embarrassment under my white make-up. I did my song again, but nobody listened at all.

By the third slot, the guests had mostly sorted themselves into couples and disappeared upstairs, and the rest were too paralytic to drag themselves in to hear us, but we'd also had so much to drink we did not mind at all.

I can definitely remember waking up and finding myself stretched out on the floor using my guitar as a pillow. My head felt like it had the previous Tuesday morning, and I groaned. Someone was snoring loudly in my left ear, and I discovered it was Devil. He certainly looked as if he'd had several over the eight – poor dog! I sat up gently, and looked round the room. It really did look as if the Bomb had actually gone off at last. Empty or broken bottles and glasses littered the place, ashtrays overflowed on the shiny tables and someone had been sick on the imitation Turkish rug near my head. People were sleeping like corpses on every sofa or armchair, and I had never wished so profoundly for my bed under the eaves as I did at that uncomfortable moment.

The butler picked his way disdainfully towards us through the debris, eyeing Devil with stern disfavour. He carried a tray of coffee, and suggested that we left as soon as possible.

Mr Zachary will be down in a few minutes,' he said and swept away like a galleon in full sail.

'I'll give him Mr Zachary,' growled Steve. 'Trust him to land in a comfortable bed.'

Zac certainly looked as cool and as crisp as ever when he finally joined us, just as we had loaded the last heavy items into the van.

'Did you enjoy it, Davo?' he asked.

'The whole night was a farce,' I growled.

'What are you on about?' he demanded. 'It was the greatest. That geezer from the recording studio said he'd let us make a demo tape, and the ITV bird said she'd work the sketch into a programme she's doing in the New Year.'

It had all sounded to me like the empty promises that people make at parties, and anyway I was quickly discovering that I hated everyone when I had a hangover.

They delivered me home at ten in the morning, so I had to hide in the bus shelter until I was sure everyone was safely in church. Devil had just bitten me, and I was frozen because I could not remember what I had done with my own clothes, when Trev had whipped his jacket and boots off me before I got out of the van. I must have looked a right wally limping painfully up the garden with a bleeding leg and bare feet. My jeans had finally split and the white greasepaint was wearing off my face, revealing my black eyes and pimples. 'Smile, Jesus loves you,' shouted my T-shirt, but it did nothing to boost my morale.

I could cheerfully have strangled Michelle. It took four frenzied attempts to get the dye out of my hair before the end of church, and even when I'd used up all Pam's shampoo my scalp stayed pink for days. I am convinced that taking the packing off my nose too soon is why it is now, not only too long, but bent as well!

Chapter Seven

Surprises

It was towards the end of dinner hour on Monday, and I was sitting in the common room with Zac. He was still full of the glories of Saturday night, and seemed in such good form I ventured to air an idea that had been churning in my mind during the night.

'I got this song Zac,' I said diffidently. 'It's about three airmen who drop their plane into the drink, and they're left with only their rubber life raft. How would it be if you lot mimed to it, while I sing? The girls could be angels and perhaps Trev could be a robot seagull or something like that.'

Zac was wildly enthusiastic.

'I've always wanted to bring the music and the drama together as a whole performance,' he said. 'We'll get everyone round to the stable tonight and give it a whirl.'

'It's only in my head still,' I said uneasily. 'Songs usually take ages to work their way down to my guitar.'

'This one's not going to,' said Zac firmly.

'We've got a concert booked for Saturday week, and we need new material. So work on it,' and with that he promptly fell asleep between two chairs.

Everyone else was outside sunbathing on the playing fields. A freak September heat wave had hit the country, after a rotten summer, and with all those winter months ahead I suppose they all wanted to make the most of the sun. But I certainly did not want to get my face tanned only on the places where the plaster was not – especially before its official removal the next day. So I was just strolling over to the vending machine to get a coffee, when the door opened and Manda hobbled in.

'Hullo David,' she said, looking oddly pleased to see me. 'I thought everyone would be at Christian Union. I hoped I'd make it but I got delayed at physio. How's your poor old nose?' She looked up at me as if she really wanted to know. Everyone else just made jokes about it. 'Someone said you'd walked into a lamppost.'

'It *was* dark,' I said stiffly. If she had been Tess I would have added, 'and I was legless at the time', but somehow I didn't want Manda to know about that. She perched herself on the edge of a table and as I stood looking down at her a strange feeling swept over me like a wave. It was not the fizzy feeling I get when I looked at Tess or even Miss Carmichael, it was just a deep almost painful need to love and be loved in return.

'David,' she said shyly, 'your Dad's asked me to do my song in church next Sunday. Please do it with me?' Her eyes looked huge in her little thin face. I'd never noticed before how lovely they were. Green with incredibly long dark lashes. Like a coward I stalled.

'You'll have a mike in church, so the PA system will do all the work for you – you won't need any help. I would spoil it.'

'Once, before all this happened I didn't know what being shy meant. I barged about not really caring what people thought. But having an accident or being ill – well it takes all your confidence away. I just don't feel I could stand up there without you.' I had a vivid mental picture of myself wrapping her tiny body in my arms and promising that she would never have to stand anywhere without me beside her for the rest of eternity. But of course I couldn't – because of Dan, and I cursed him under my breath. So I compromised by taking her hand and holding it a great deal more tightly than necessary.

'Look,' I said, 'there's something I've got to tell you.' I longed for her to think well of me and understand how I was feeling, but I hated to have to explain to her. 'I can't go to church any more.' She gazed up at me – stunned.

'Not ever?' she said. 'Why?'

'I think I've outgrown Christianity,' I said trying to sound sophisticated like Zac. She dropped my hand as if it had been dirty.

'You haven't outgrown it David,' she said, as two bright spots of colour appeared on her cheeks. 'You're not enough of a man to dare to be a Christian. It takes a lot of guts these days – especially in places like Gravely. You're just a baby, that's your trouble.' I felt stung all over and stepping backwards I fell unceremoniously over a chair. It was one thing to have Steve calling me an effeminate runt, but this was Manda talking.

'I've seen you,' she continued relentlessly, as I picked myself up. 'Creeping around after Zac's lot. They'll never accept you. It's only your voice they want, not you. Oh! how I wish you'd just grow up.' Great tears were trickling down her face, and grabbing her stick she jerked herself out of the room.

'I'd say that bird fancies you,' said a sleepy voice from the chairs in the corner, but just for once I did *not* believe Zac Farroudi.

The new song turned out to be very funny with the marooned airmen being eaten by gorgeously attractive cannibals (Michelle and Tess) on a desert island. Zac insisted that we gave it a women's lib twist, but with Zac as one of the airmen and Monkey a gorilla, it really was hilarious.

61

The week shot by as we worked every night in the stables. Zac was always at his very best when working on a new project. He activated us all as if we had been model airplanes flying by remote control. I watched him fascinated – he used up so much nervous energy during one of those evenings, that it was no wonder he was like a zapped zombie at school.

I knew that he was pleased with the way I was improving their sound, but I still felt the others did not accept me.

Wherever I went that week I was conscious of curious glances. At school a lot of the CU had lived off me like spiritual parasites, now they watched me and the Anarchists with hurt, bewildered eyes.

'But what about your homework?' Mum would lament when I told her I was going out for yet another evening. But I knew the crunch would come on Sunday morning. No one who lives at the Manse ever misses church, not unless they are actually ill in bed. First Mum called upstairs. 'Breakfast Davy, you're late.'

'Pity,' I thought as I turned over and put a pillow over my head. It was always hot rolls and honey on Sunday morning. Mum thinks Sundays should be a 'do' day and not full of 'don'ts', so we had lots of little treats throughout the day – but hot rolls and honey were the best. Then Dad stuck his head round the door when he came out of the top bathroom.

'You'll be late for church, old boy,' he said. 'I'm just off now.'

'Come on Davy,' said Mum ten minutes later, 'this isn't like you.'

'I'm not going,' I said from under the pillow. There was such a long silence I had to remove my head in the end and confront her face to face.

'I'm not going to church ever again.' Pain shot across her

face as if I had hit her, and she sank down on to the end of my bed.

'Look, there's a whole churchful of people over there,' she said. 'This is the third week you've missed, what are they going to think?'

'I don't care what they think,' I replied, trying to sound as rude as I could.

'But we're a team Davy,' she said. 'You, me and Dad — the Youth Group is built up round you.'

'I don't want to be part of your team any more,' I spat. 'I want to stand on my own.'

'But all the young people look up to you,' she quavered.

'I'm fed up with being "looked up to", and typecast for life,' I said and retreated back under my pillow, and I heard her patter sadly away. It is so maddening, wanting to quarrel with someone who won't quarrel back!

I lay in bed planning what I would do if Mum and Dad really got tough and tried to stop my new way of life.

'I'll leave home,' I thought, 'sleep rough in Zac's stable. They probably wouldn't even notice I'd gone.' But underneath I knew Dad was giving me enough rope to hang myself, and the thought of that, coupled with the fact that I was depriving myself of the chance to gaze at Manda while she sang her new song in church, did nothing to improve my temper.

I think it must have been later that day that I had rather a shock. I had to go to the stable for a practice after lunch, and Mum asked me to drop a letter into someone's house on the way. 'Miss Williams, 16 Sherbrook Avenue', said the envelope, and I felt annoyed. All those new housing estates looked the same, I was bound to get lost. After a good deal of hassle, I was just pushing the letter through the ridiculously small letter box and pitying all postmen, when I heard a door bang violently round the side of the house, and angry, but rather unsteady footsteps coming up the path. Suddenly there was Manda – her green eyes positively glinting with rage. I'd heard that people with red hair had hot tempers, and I could not help thinking how magnificent she looked when she was angry.

'Whatever's bugged you?' I grinned.

'Parents!' she replied attacking the geraniums vigorously with her walking stick. 'There's lots of books written about difficult teenagers. When's someone going to write one about bringing up parents? It's hard enough being disabled, without having to be kept in cotton wool like an exhibit in a museum.'

'Cool down,' I soothed, 'you'll blow a gasket.'

'Mum always was a fusser,' she continued, lowering her voice, 'but since my accident she's gone paranoid. "Don't do that, it'll tire you, dear", or "why don't you go and have a lie down". I'm sick of it – that's not living!'

'I'm a bit fed up with my parents at present,' I said, 'but I never thought that you . . .'

'What do you think I am then – some kind of a saint?'

'Well, yes I did really,' I faltered. Suddenly she seemed to crumble, and rather pathetically she flopped down on her garden wall.

'I'm no saint,' she said miserably, 'and tomorrow Dan's going off to college, and I wish I was dead.'

The afternoon sun was playing about with her curls and without thinking I reached out to touch one, but just at that moment Dan drove up in his father's car, and Manda was whisked away from me again. What a fool I was ever to dream she could be mine.

Chapter Eight

A Step Backwards

'Have a good day,' smiled Mum as she handed us our sandwiches.

'And don't work too hard,' added Dad as he watched Pam slipping her dark glasses and suntan oil into her school bag. We were off for a day trip to Brighton – supposedly to study urban land use and settlement patterns for our geography course project, but with the heat wave still holding we could all think of better ways to use a day by the sea. I was not feeling pleased with Pam that morning. I had nurtured a happy daydream in which I had escorted Manda round Brighton all day, only to have the whole thing shattered when I discovered that Manda had consented to use a wheelchair for the day which Pam, Dominic and hordes of the CU were intending to push. I sensed that she would hate it, and I knew for sure that I would never get a look in.

It really is horrid arriving on board a coach and not having anyone to sit next to. The Anarchists had naturally bagged the back seat, and they did not look like making room for even a runt like me. Tess was on her own, but when I tried to slide in beside her, she said, 'Shove off, this is reserved for Zac.' I certainly did not want to sit next to any of my old friends in case they asked me why I had not been to church lately, and even Miss Carmichael seemed to prefer the bus driver's company.

I pretended to be deeply absorbed in my book and tried not to feel like a displaced person.

The coach was just pulling out of the main school gate when it stopped suddenly with a gasp from its air brakes.

'You're late Zachary Farroudi,' snapped Miss Carmichael crossly as he pulled himself up the steps.

'I had to pop back home for my bikini,' he said smiling down at her. 'I hope you've remembered yours Miss Carmichael.' If I had said that it would have sounded cheeky, but he had the power to melt all females, and this one was no exception.

Tess was patting the spare seat beside her so invitingly that I was amazed when Zac swung in beside me. He looked ghastly, with huge bags under his bloodshot eyes.

'I had a bottle or two too many last night,' he said. 'Thanks for rescuing me from the predator – she would have swallowed me whole before we got halfway to Brighton.' Certainly Tess was biting the air at us from over the gangway and tossing her mane in a very lion-like manner, but Zac was fast asleep again, so her performance was lost on him entirely.

We had quite a job shaking her off in Brighton when we finally arrived there, and were only delivered by a gents toilet that had a side door into another street.

'I need a drink!' said Zac when he realised we were actually free of her at last, and he dived into an Off Licence.

'Oughtn't we to start work now?' I asked, clutching my clipboard on which was the mapped route we were supposed to follow.

'Work?' he said, emptying a small bottle of whisky down his throat like a baby blackbird welcoming a worm. 'Work, on a day like this? You've got to be joking Davo. We'll copy off one of the girls on the way home. Let your fingers do the walking, that's my motto.'

66

As the fresh air dealt with his hangover, I realised what fun he was to be with, and we happily talked shop as we mooched about the little streets they call Lanes and poked into all the dusty junk shops.

'We should get a full house on Saturday. We're supporting Blue Magic, and they're very well known,' he said as he tried on an old Air Force leather flying jacket. 'I'll wear this for the new sketch,' he added peeling off a wad of fivers from the fat bundle in his wallet and poking them over the counter. 'I'm really pleased with the way that's shaping up, Davo, you've really got the touch.'

'What do you think I should wear?' I asked, rather bleakly. 'The lead singer should always dress up a bit,' he said. 'You looked very cool in Trev's stuff. Can't you get hold of some gear like that?' I had an allowance of ten pounds a month to buy all my own clothes, and there was no point in asking Dad for any more. He never had any money, and even when he did, he always gave it away to the first lame dog who limped along. But I wasn't going to say all that to Zac. I'd just have to get hold of some money somehow.

'I'm starved,' he said suddenly as we passed a Wimpy. 'Let's get some grub.' Mum had given me 30p for a coffee and my usual school sandwiches, but I could not tell him that either. I was beginning to value his friendship so highly I did not want to let myself down. So I had to sit there and watch him tuck into a huge steak and chips while I nibbled surreptitiously from my bag under the table.

'Waitress? Same again please,' said Zac suddenly. When I go into a cafe I always seem to be invisible to waitresses, but Zac is the kind of person who only had to lift an eyebrow and they come running from all directions.

'You're never going to eat two like that,' I said in awed envy.

'No, this one's for you,' he said casually. 'I'm fed up with you watching every chip from my plate to my mouth.'

'I don't want your charity,' I blazed. 'Just 'cos you're dirty rich . . .'

'Cool it man,' said Zac lazily, 'I've got to get some muscle on that runt body of yours – it's a manager's job.' I was still cross but the steak did taste good.

'I need a drink,' said Zac yet again as he paid our bill from his ever-obliging wallet. 'Let's head back to that Off Licence.'

'You drink more than anyone else I know,' I laughed. But Zac was not laughing when he replied, 'I know someone who drank more than me – my Mum, and a long way it got her too,' he added bitterly. 'She was soaked most of the time, that's one of the reasons why . . .'

'Why she left you?' I asked.

'No,' he replied bleakly, 'there was another, bigger reason,' and he shuddered as if he was remembering something very horrible. 'I suppose I'm hooked now,' he finished miserably, 'the same as she was. I feel so bad about it I have to keep on drinking to forget it.'

'But you said you can't act unless you're legless,' I said. This was a new side of Zac that he had never shown me before.

'At first it does help me,' he admitted. 'But after a certain point it takes control of me and ruins the act. Trouble is, I never know when I've reached that point, and even if I did know, I doubt if I could just stop – I'm just plain hooked and it scares me.'

He disappeared once more into the Off Licence and when he came out again he seemed to have shaken off his gloomy mood, and it was then that we saw them – two punks in gorgeous leather jackets and sharply pointed calf-length boots.

'That's the look I want, Zac,' I said. 'All those chains and amulets would hide my Adam's apple.'

He shouted with laughter. 'You don't want to be a punk, do you?' he said.

'I don't really care,' I growled. 'I just want to be somebody else.'

'Then *act* the part of somebody else,' he replied suddenly serious.

'Is life just a play then?' I asked bitterly.

'What else should it be, man?' he answered. 'Go and buy yourself punk gear if that's what you want.' Oh *why* could he not understand what it felt like not to be able to do that?

Trev had got his stuff without paying for it. But I couldn't steal. Or could I? If there was no God to say 'thou shalt not steal', then what was to stop me taking what I needed? But I'd never be brave enough, and just suppose I got caught?

'What's up?' asked Zac, 'you look like you're riding off to your own funeral.' I shivered and the two punks walked away from us down the Lane that led to the sea.

'Come on, let's follow them,' said Zac. 'I suppose we ought to get a bit of a suntan.'

'You've already been in films, haven't you?' I asked as we sauntered along the crowded promenade.

'Three,' he replied. 'The first one was a horror film and I was seven when I did that. I had to be eaten by a monster, and I got out of school for a whole term for that one. As soon as I get out of Gravely I'm going into films for good. Dad's got lots of contacts, but I don't just want to act – I'm going to produce the greatest films ever made.

As we walked along in the hot sun, I suddenly had the strange certainty that he liked me. I could not think why on earth someone like him who had every single thing going for him could possibly like someone who looked like a woodpecker with dish-mop legs.

69

It was almost as if he read my thoughts because he suddenly said, 'Do you remember our first week at Gravely?'

'Yeh,' I grinned, 'we were all in our stiff new blazers with creases down our trousers!'

'Tess had pigtails and Michelle had a brace on her teeth,' added Zac.

'Poor old Monkey was still wearing his little Yiddish skullcap. He used to take some knocks for that. Steve was always pulling those long black curls he had to have down the sides of his face! That's the first thing I remember about you Davo. Steve was kicking Monkey round in the First Year playground, and you were such a little shrimp, smallest kid in the school, yet you stood in front of Monkey and said, "Lay off him, he's one of God's chosen people." Everyone cracked up, but I've never forgotten that.'

I had, and it didn't sound very much like me, except that I remember being very fervent when young!

'I've been watching you ever since, wondering if there's anything in this religious bug after all.'

'Well there's not,' I said crossly. 'It's only a tranquillizer for old ladies.'

Zac said no more, but his silence felt vaguely disappointed.

We were sitting dangling our legs over the prom and eating huge icecreams – thanks to the generosity of Mr Farroudi, when we saw the two punks again – on the beach, this time, right under our feet.

'They must be hot inside those jackets,' I said, wiping the sweat from my own forehead in sympathy.

'They never take them off,' laughed Zac. 'They're a status symbol.' But he was wrong.

'I'm cooking,' said the shorter one of the two. 'I've gotta

70

get into that sea even if I ruin my hairdo. You stay here and watch the gear.' And soon he was speeding across the shingle as eagerly as a lemming in his underpants. Suddenly the other one appeared to be taken violently short. He gazed round the beach wildly and then dashed in the direction of the gents.

There at my feet, not two metres away lay all that I needed to alter my minister's son image for ever – free for the taking. No one would notice me, as they all lay basking in the drowsy afternoon sunshine.

'Well, God's boy, what about it?' Zac's eyes were challenging me. For a split second I gazed at him, and then without another thought I jumped down on to the beach, whipped the jacket and boots into the Tesco bag on top of my half-eaten picnic and was back up beside him before a seagull could have uttered a protest.

'Let's get out of here,' he said out of the corner of his mouth. 'But don't run, play it cool man.' Was I imagining it, or did he look disappointed? Had he expected something different from me?

Hastily we left the beach behind us and took cover in the rabbit warren that were the Lanes. I could still hear my heart beating right up in my ears, and it was not until I was perfectly sure there were no angry feet pounding behind us, that I began to realise what I had done. Suddenly we emerged from the secretive shadows of the alleyways, and came out through an archway into a square courtyard of sun-drenched shops. A group of people were sitting round a little fountain in the middle of the square, talking and laughing just as if the whole world belonged to them. Suddenly Manda separated herself from them and came propelling her wheelchair at high speed over the pavings towards us.

'Have you finished already?' she laughed.

'Finished?' grinned Zac. 'We haven't even started yet.'
As he smiled down at her, something inside my chest began
to hurt me badly. Would she manage to resist his charm
where all other females had failed?

'What's the guilty secret you're clutching in the Tesco
bag David?' she teased, and I gasped wondering if she had
x-ray eyes.

'Just swimming stuff,' I muttered. I had taken a very
definite step away from God and all I had ever lived for in
my whole life, and now the gulf between me and this girl I
loved had become too wide for any bridge ever to span.

Chapter Nine

A Transformation

It was hot and stuffy in my bedroom under the eaves that night. I tried to tell myself I was feeling great. I had done something really brave and clever for the first time in my life, but I kept remembering the only other time that I had ever stolen anything in my life. It had been a tulip from a neighbour's garden to give to Mum as a present. She had been very sweet about it, but she had made me take it back.

'But the Anarchists would accept me, if only I looked right,' I argued. 'I must have an identity.' But I had not finished acquiring mine yet. I pulled a face at myself in the mirror. My hair still looked like something from Eton or Harrow. I needed a really good new style, but the 80p I had left from that month's allowance would not even pay for a short back and sides. I had gone so far now, I could not leave myself half finished. I must get hold of some money somehow. It was then that I thought about the Thursday collection.

'No way!' I told myself firmly. 'That belongs to the church.' It was one thing to pinch second-hand clothes, but quite another to rob God (if He existed) – that was going too far. But didn't the church owe it to me really? After all, if they had only paid Dad a decent salary he could have given me a bigger allowance. It was the church's fault I was being tempted like this.

I pushed the thought out of my head, but it kept creeping

back. The whole thing would be so easy to do. So many people came to those Thursday evening Bible studies who were not connected with our church and they liked to contribute towards our expenses; and people paid for the tapes in advance. Dad brought the collection bag home with him, but he was always so tired on a Thursday evening that he just put it down on his desk with his Bible and forgot about it. Mum was always on at him. 'With so many people in and out of the Manse all day – anyone could help themselves,' she would say.

I went round during that Wednesday and Thursday, in a churn of indecision. The old and the new David were fighting one another to the death, but as I went to sleep on the Thursday night, the new David had won. I did not dare to rouse the whole house by using my alarm clock, so I willed myself to wake at 3 in the morning – and I did.

I could hear John snoring through the wall, and I wondered if he ever belched in his sleep. I could not put a light on, but I managed to get downstairs without breaking my nose again, and I felt my way across the study, until I encountered Dad's desk.

I drew the curtains a little so the moonlight could help me see what I was doing, and then I began to transfer the treasure trove into my dressing gown pockets. Once I heard a creak from overhead, and I froze, but it must only have been one of the mums getting a drink for her baby – John's snores could be heard right down here. I could not help wishing the moonlight was not streaming in through the window right on to Dad's open Bible; it felt horribly as if God was watching me.

But when I counted my takings in the streaky pink light of early dawn, I found I had £60 – that was a fortune to me, and I hid it under the carpet at the back of my bed. Mum could hardly be described as house-proud, and she never hoovers under beds, but all the same I went down to breakfast feeling a little apprehensive. Dad would have spent at least two hours sitting at his desk reading his Bible that morning. Surely he would have realised the collection bag had gone on a diet. But Dad's mind is on higher things, and he was as irritatingly cheerful as people are when they get up two hours before breakfast.

I did not exactly rush home from school. In fact, I positively loitered over the common, guessing that Dad would probably have discovered the loss of the collection money just before three-thirty, when he always remembered he ought to have gone to the bank. So by now, a clear hour later, the fat would surely be in the fire, and I was right. To say the atmosphere in our kitchen was strained was a ludicrous understatement.

A huge police sergeant sat bulging out of his uniform in Dad's chair by the Aga, an ominous notebook in his hand. The entire household was assembled including the babies, who were squawking hopefully for their tea. The whole scene reminded me of the last chapter in an Agatha Christie murder.

'Something terrible has happened, Davy,' said Mum as I pushed open the back door. Her face was a hectic scarlet, but Dad was as white as his dog collar.

I will not be such a fine actor as Zac, but I think I gave a very good performance that afternoon as I allowed surprise, concern and then outrage to pass across my face in turn. I had been running through my part all day. Poor old George had been 'inside' a few times before Mum took him in hand, and his chin was wagging up and down in helpless agitation. John, being an ex-junkie naturally felt he was under suspicion, and Pam was on probation for shoplifting, so the vibes in the room were rather powerful.

'Look, sergeant,' said Mum wiping her burning face with

damp kitchen paper, 'we're having a jumble sale in the church hall tomorrow, and people have been in and out all day, delivering stuff, and we store it all in the study. It could have been one of at least twenty people who've been here today.'

'But more likely to have been someone who knew it was there,' said the policeman doggedly, and his bloodshot eye rolled in my direction suspiciously.

'I haven't asked *this* young lad any questions yet,' he said ominously.

'This is my son,' laughed Dad. 'He's quite above suspicion. I would trust him with everything I possess.'

The sergeant did not look very convinced, and I felt smaller than I had ever felt in my life before. 'Is there anyone in this house who is urgently in need of money?' went on the policeman relentlessly. Pam burst into tears and John belched loudly.

'Look, sergeant,' said Dad, 'all this is my fault. I ought to have had more sense. I should have locked the money away. I'll make it up from my own pocket. I can't have my household getting upset,' and he put a protecting arm round Pam's shoulders and gave George a reassuring pat.

The policeman looked doubtful. 'It seems a shame to let the culprit get away with it,' he said sourly. 'I suppose you'll be letting your church committee know? Perhaps they'll see fit to install some kind of a safe. If any further evidence comes to light, you will let me know won't you?'

Dad promised hastily, and hustled him towards the door.

I knew how much it would hurt Dad's pocket to pay out £60 and I was not acting when I blazed, 'Why should *you* find the money Dad? The church should pay!'

'The Lord will provide,' smiled Dad, but I knew Mum would probably have to help the Lord a bit by feeding us all on spaghetti and potatoes for the next few months. I felt a frightful heel, but it was too late to put the money back then.

Supper in the Manse that night was not the noisy affair it usually was. George never spoke a word, and Pam did not giggle once. However, John made up for them by burping more horrifically than I think he ever has before. Whether that was due to shock or because Mum had burnt the potatoes black and stuck the stew to the bottom of the saucepan, I shall never know.

When Saturday morning came, I knew exactly where I was heading. There was a certain trendy barber in town whose partner did tattooing and ear piercing, and by ten o'clock I was on my way. I had managed to get out of the house wearing my new jacket and boots, plus all my necklaces, chains and bracelets – and no one saw me, which was a miracle in itself. I was feeling particularly pleased because the night before, while sorting through the mounds of smelly jumble in the study, I had discovered a pair of jeans that fitted me like a drainpipe.

I emerged from the barber's shop after several hours and I only had enough change to buy a can of beer. The minister's son was left behind in the shop like an empty chrysalis, and out into the sunshine strode 'Davo the Daring'.

'My dear boy! what have you done?' It was unfortunate that 'Davo the Daring', being too proud to look where he was going collided violently with the church treasurer. The poor little man, who had known me since babyhood gazed in horror, lost his footing on the edge of the pavement, and would have landed in the gutter if I had not grabbed him in time. I suppose I must have given him quite a shock. My head was shaved except for a luminous green fringe sticking up along the middle. On either side of the shiny white skull were large tattoos, a spread eagle on the left and a coiled serpent on the right. Large rings pierced my ears, and I had a smaller one in my misshapen nose. As I swaggered home enjoying the startled expression of the people I met, I really could not have looked more different from the boy I had been a week before. Of course, *now* I would have been hopelessly out of fashion, but I felt right in at the front that day.

I don't think that I had stopped to consider what effect the 'new me' would have on my parents, and I arrived at the Manse just as they were both climbing into their terrible old banger, to do their weekly hospital visiting. Dad stopped dead, one arm and one leg in the car while the other half of him froze on the driveway, and Mum dropped her Little Red Riding Hood basket of goodies with an unnoticed thud on the rose bed.

'Well, at least you've noticed that I exist,' I thought, mentally clenching my fists. Now at least we could have that long awaited fight. But Dad never said a word, he just stood there taking in every detail and you could see him doing sums in his head. Click, click, click, two and two make four.

'It was you who took the collection money, wasn't it?' It was not a question or an accusation, just a statement of fact.

'What if I did?' I sneered. 'If you got yourself a proper job with a decent salary, I wouldn't have had to spend my life looking like a Sunday school prize. I know you won't shop me,' I added bitterly, 'the publicity might damage your image. You only want to use me as an object lesson. "If you bring up your children as well as I've brought up mine, they too will turn out as beautifully as our little Davy." Well I'm fed up with being the prize marrow at the church fete.'

Mum climbed rather quickly into the car, and put her hands over her eyes. I longed for Dad to shout back as startled faces appeared in every window of the Manse, but he just looked stricken, shrivelled and old.

'I love you so much, Davy,' he said, groping towards me with a shaking hand. 'I really do love you.'

I shrugged his hand from my shoulder, 'Don't keep on calling me Davy,' I spat, 'I'm not your baby any more.' I turned my back on them and stamped into the house, slamming the front door with as much force as I could muster. If Dad could have seen me five minutes later, he might have been very surprised. I was lying face down on my bed crying like the baby I had just declared I no longer was – but Dad was far too busy driving off to the Police Station.

Chapter Ten

Reactions

I shall never forget the gigantic shock I received that afternoon. It never entered my head that Dad would really do it. I thought Mum was calling me down to tea, but when she diverted me into the study and I found myself gazing at that bullfrog of a sergeant, I just about fainted with surprise.

He looked me up and down from the tip of my green fringe to the pointed toe of my expensive boots, and remarked sarcastically, 'Well, you've been spending a good bit of money in the last few days, and you're the one who was "above suspicion".' Dad stood miserably behind the sergeant's chair, and Mum handed him a cup of tea and such a huge slice of chocolate cake that I wondered if it was a bribe or a threat.

'And where may I ask did you find all the money for all that get-up?' I was so irritated by his cat and mouse game, that I eyed him coldly and said, 'I took the collection money.'

'You're not denying it then?' said the sergeant sounding rather disappointed. I shook my head – and it felt odd without its hair.

'Well then, Reverend,' he continued cramming his mouth full of cake, 'you told me down at the station that you have already paid the sixty pounds that were missing. Presumably you'll be seeing your church deacons about this latest development,' he added pointedly, 'but if they don't wish to press charges, then there's nothing more we can do.' The thought seemed to upset him so much, he asked for another slice of cake.

When we were finally rid of him, Dad groped his way over to the telephone on his desk. 'I'll have to convene an emergency elders' meeting after the service tomorrow,' he said miserably. He looked so stricken that I suddenly realised that if I had wanted to punish him for ignoring me I could not have found a more painful way of doing it. He was going to be shamed in front of people who respected and admired him.

'Dad,' I gulped, 'I went into the newsagent's yesterday — they're advertising a paper round, and I got the job. I'll give you all I earn.' I couldn't manage to say sorry, but he knew that's what I meant, and his tense face suddenly relaxed.

'I'm sorry I couldn't cover up for you,' he said apologetically, 'but I had to prove to you that I loved you more than my public image.' When Dad laughs, it's impossible not to laugh with him, however hard you try not to.

The next few days were traumatic, and that's putting it mildly. I felt just the same inside, so the reactions of other people to my changed appearance came as a fresh shock each time. I had fondly hoped that the Anarchists would accept me now, but when Big Jim brought their van to a screeching halt outside the Manse that night, there was a startled silence as I swung myself in through the door.

'What have you *done* to yourself, runt?' gasped Steve, and Devil growled as if I had been a stranger.

'I can't believe anyone could be that *stupid*!' said Monkey. Simon polished his glasses in order to take a better look at me, and Jim seemed unable to drive off, he just sat staring at me in horror.

'Look,' said Monkey as if he was explaining something to

a very small child. 'Because the drama is our main thing, we try to keep the music as neutral as possible, so we can appeal to all tastes. We can't have a way out punk as a lead singer or lots of our gigs wouldn't book us.'

'But lots of others would,' put in Zac thoughtfully.

'What are you on about?' frowned Steve.

'It might pay us to have him a punk in some places,' explained Zac, 'but on other nights you'll just have to wear a wig Davo – develop a flexible image.'

'But tonight was going to be our big break,' wailed Michelle. 'What are we going to do?'

'We'll make them laugh at him,' said Zac with sudden decision. 'Make his face up as a clown Michelle, and we'll pop back to the stable for that false nose with a red light bulb in it.'

'I could rig up a switch on the sole of his shoe,' put in Simon, his eye gleaming with anticipation, 'then he could light up his nose in time to the beat.'

Suddenly we heard an extraordinary noise coming from the back of the van – it was Trev laughing. I never knew he could. 'Just think,' he spluttered, 'when you're a famous preacher like your Dad, you'll get old and go bald and everyone in church will see your eagle and the serpent.'

I did not feel much like 'Davo the Daring' standing on the stage of Maidford Town Hall that night, but the audience loved me. My new sketch was a huge success, but we all agreed it was my flashing nose that got us the most future bookings.

I was acutely embarrassed at Sunday lunch next day by the intent gaze of one of the babies who seemed to be so fascinated by my Mohawkan fringe he was unable to eat a thing. Suddenly, during an unusual lull in the conversation, he pointed a fat finger in my direction and said 'Cockadoodledoo'. Everyone all round the crowded table collapsed with laughter, while I stalked from the room. But as I passed my old friend the mirror, I had to admit I no longer looked like a woodpecker – I certainly did resemble a cockerel.

'What are *you* doing here?' demanded the fat little man in the newsagents when I arrived to start my new job at six o'clock on Monday morning.

'I've come to do my paper round,' I faltered.

The little man looked me up and down in disgust, 'I thought you were Reverend Martin's boy,' he said, 'not a layabout.'

I would like to have said that a layabout would hardly have turned up for work at that ghastly hour of the morning, and he could stuff his papers down his own fat throat, but I needed that job for Dad's sake, so I managed to pick up my bag of papers in meek silence, and save my richer language until I was safely out of the shop.

All that was only a pinprick in comparison with the strain of arriving at Gravely three hours later. It wasn't that I was the only punk, even Mr King Canute Atkins had given up trying to stem the tide of Mohawkans, it was the dramatic change in *me* that made people lose their false teeth gaping. The CU obviously thought I was not quite beyond their help, and the other punks hooted at me derisively, knowing that I was not really one of them. For someone who had spent all their life trying to merge into the background suddenly to find they were the school sensation, was enough to make 'Davo the Daring' wish the disinfected school floors would open and swallow him – nose ring and all.

Only one person went out of their way to talk to me as if I was still a human being, and that was Manda. Perhaps she knew only too well how it feels to be stared at, and I loved her for caring. But since that day in Brighton, I had never been able to look her straight in the face.

'David Martin, come out here.' It was the beginning of our class period and I had been dreading Miss Carmichael's reaction. She walked round me twice, eyeing me from every angle while I stood feeling horribly conspicuous at the front of the class.

'Good,' she said at last. 'It's the next step.'

'Next step?' I repeated blankly.

'You've spent years trying to look like your father, now you're copying someone else. One day you'll have the guts to look like yourself, then you'll have grown up. This is an improvement. I used to think you were nothing but a smug little prig.'

I have already said that Manda has a hot temper, and says things without thinking first.

'That's not fair, Miss Carmichael,' she blazed. 'Just because someone's a Christian, doesn't mean they're prigs.'

'I didn't say that,' frowned Miss Carmichael. 'When I meet people who are "genuine" Christians, like David's father, they shake my ideas about badly, but David was only ever pretending.' I was livid with her, mostly because I knew she was right. But Monkey jumped into the boiling pot before I could defend myself.

'Genuine Christians, bagh!' he spat, 'they cause nothing but trouble.'

'Yes,' put in Steve, 'look what "Christians" did to Mary Jenkins last year – stoned her for a witch.'

'They weren't genuine Christians,' stormed Manda, 'they were the sham kind.'

Miss Carmichael called the class to order, but I couldn't help realising that Manda too was going through an identity change. Her confidence was returning rapidly. When Mary Jenkins had been at Gravely, she had been hated and feared, as too had Manda, but since Mary had left, a cult had grown up round her memory. Anyone who was interested in the occult or Satan worship were constantly discussing her and the stories of her powers lost nothing in the telling.

When Manda had first come back to school again, and everyone had got over the shock of seeing her so changed, she had become quite a celebrity, and clusters of people were always round asking her questions about witchcraft and pestering her for more information.

At first, I could see that it worried her and then quite suddenly her shyness dropped away, and with Dan off the stage she could be a person in her own right. When people asked her about the occult, she turned the conversation round to Christianity and it was not long before she got the nickname, 'Billy Graham'. I felt oddly proud of her, but yet, if there was a God, why wasn't she angry with Him?

Chapter Eleven

Manda Rises to the Occasion

Mr Scot was a Nazi, well that's what people said. I'd never thought about him as a person, to me he was just a very fine history teacher: but as I sat at the back of his classroom one muggy November day, I could quite see how he got his reputation. He must have been in his late forties, but his hair was still strikingly blond and his blue eyes glowed out of a handsome Germanic face. If you put him in a black uniform he would be perfect as an SS officer in a war film.

Thinking like this was the only way of distracting my mind from the lesson he was teaching. I had always been fascinated by history; in fact, it had been my best subject, and I was finding it much harder *not* to work hard than it had been to excel.

I ran my fingers through my ever-lengthening green fringe, and realised that people had got used to my new look much more quickly than I had adjusted to my new way of life. The safe little cocooned world which had almost entirely consisted of reading books or playing my battered wooden guitar had been ripped open, and I felt I had been sucked into the centre of a whirlwind. I never had a minute to breathe these days.

We almost lived in the stable, working up new songs and sketches, and because they blended together so uniquely, we were much in demand, for there was no other group in the district doing anything remotely like that. We were out several times in the week as well as every weekend.

Mr Scot's voice kept demanding to be heard. The lesson was on the Rise of Hitler and the Third Reich, a particular interest of mine, so I gripped my ruler and practised microphone technique – anything to distract my mind. I was working on my yodel, but you have to be just the right distance from the mike for that, or the audience run for the doors. I shut my eyes and tried to imagine what I must look like on stage, standing there in a pool of light – unseen eyes watching from the darkness. Of course, I would never manage Steve's antics. He held his guitar like a machine gun and jabbed it aggressively at the audience, but my latest trick of whirling my left arm like a windmill was getting very popular with our fans.

I loved the gigs where I could be a punk and hated the 'smooth image' evenings. Zac made me wear a curly blond wig then, which was tethered to my head by a silver sweat band which matched the stripes in my trousers.

Yes, we were certainly looking and sounding much better these days, and we were even beginning to make money. But where did it all go? I sighed. Michelle did my hair for me each week which was a saving, but I was drinking heavily by then, and smoking as well, so I had to take on a double paper round, and even demeaned myself to work in that dirty little shop on Saturdays.

Even then I could not afford the kind of clothes Zac wore, and I minded about that, so I took some lessons from Trev and became quite good at shoplifting.

I yawned; it was hot in that classroom. I glanced across the aisle at Monkey. He looked white as paper and was shaking all over. 'I suppose it's the strain of life,' I thought, it was telling on all of us. The only time I wasn't tired out was when I was on stage. But if I wanted money to buy all the expensive things I longed for, I must get to the top of the pop world.

My eyes strayed to the front of the class where Manda was sitting, and I felt a dull ache somewhere under my blazer pocket. I had composed so many love songs about her, and sung them to thousands of other girls, but she had never heard one of them. Would money and fame ever be a substitute for her love?

Something was definitely very wrong with Monkey. He looked like a rocket gushing white vapour on the launching pad, preparing for take-off.

'Hitler was one of the greatest leaders the world has ever known,' Mr Scot's voice was vibrating with something oddly like hero worship. 'Don't ever forget,' he continued, 'history books are written by the victors whose accounts are often distorted and inaccurate. One day, when all this emotional hysteria has subsided, Hitler will be allowed to take his rightful place in human estimation.'

Suddenly the rocket on my left completed its countdown.

'How dare you!' shouted Monkey leaping to his feet, and I remembered that he was a Jew.

Mr Scot's Aryan blue eyes narrowed and his mouth contracted into a cruel line. Suddenly I began to recall history lessons back through all our years at Gravely. I had often wondered why Mr Scot picked so systematically on Monkey. Most of the Yiddish community in Fleetbridge went to their own private school, so was Monkey the only Jew in his power?

'You don't know what you're talking about,' said Monkey trying to control his voice. 'My grandparents died in Auschwitz, and my mother was born in there.'

'You Jews are always snivelling with self-pity,' sneered Mr Scott, and the explosion inside Monkey launched his rocket at last, and he shot out of his desk. Something ugly was going to happen: danger has an unmistakeable smell. Monkey lunged up the narrow aisle towards Mr Scot, who stood smirking at the front, luring him on to destruction. I knew there was something I ought to do, but while I was wondering what it was, Manda had done it. From her place in the front row she stumbled into Monkey's murderous path, effectually barring his way. I leapt to my feet fearing he would knock her down, but her words paralysed us all.

'Mr Scot, wasn't your father shot for war crimes after his trial at Nuremberg?' Her voice was very quiet. Mr Scot looked as startled as if he had been shot like his father. 'You started life as Carl Schultz, didn't you?' continued Manda, from her precarious position between the two antagonists. 'You didn't become Charles Scot until you were six and your mother married a British serviceman.'

Mr Scot swallowed hard and gave Manda a look of pure loathing. 'They *said* that you had changed since your accident, but I can see you are still the same gossiping little toad that you were last year. That revolting Mary Jenkins discovered all that, and made me pay to keep it quiet. You haven't changed at all.'

Manda seemed to crumple and shrank back into her place. 'I'm sorry,' she whispered, 'I had no right to use that information, but I had to stop you picking on Monkey all the time.'

'If my parents were to make a formal complaint,' spat Monkey, 'in the light of who you are, I doubt if it would do your career much good.'

'This class is dismissed,' hissed Mr Scot, and clicked smartly out of the room, leaving a stunned silence behind him.

I was at Manda's side before Monkey had time to thank her, but she was biting her lip and looked very close to tears.

'I promised God I'd never use any of the things Mary discovered,' she sobbed. 'I wanted to be free of that old life.'

'*God!*' sneered Monkey. 'How could He possibly exist?'

'I thought you were a Jew,' I said jumping in on Manda's side without a second thought.

'Just because I was *born* a Jew, doesn't mean I have to be one by religion,' sneered Monkey. 'I despise my parents for believing in a God who allowed the Holocaust. They *say* we're His chosen people and He gave us the Land of Israel, so why did He kick us out of it for two thousand years, to be murdered and despised all round the world?'

'Because you killed His son,' said Garry. He's a member of the Christian Union, and he is usually so quiet, it was quite a surprise to find he had a voice.

'Bagh! Jesus Christ,' sneered Monkey, 'you goys have been using him as a weapon against us for centuries.'

'But ever since Abraham, God promised you a Messiah,' I heard myself saying. 'Just suppose Jesus Christ *was* who He said He was, don't you think God would be rather upset when you crucified Him?'

'Thought you didn't believe in God any more, Davo,' drawled a lazy voice behind me. Zac, who was certainly *not* in the top set for history, must have come into the room without being noticed and I wondered how long he had been standing behind me.

'All right,' spat Monkey aggressively. 'So why did He give us back our land again? So He could rub our noses in it?'

I wanted to reply, but I was too conscious of Zac standing there, and it was Manda who filled in the gap. 'He's giving your nation another chance,' she said simply. 'He's always doing that kind of thing. If He didn't, wherever would I be?'

'Will you get your parents to complain about Mr Scot?' asked Garry.

'If I even mention him to them, they would make me go to the Yiddish school. Anyway, we Jews never complain – what's the point,' he added bitterly, and slouched out of the room to withdraw into one of his fits of melancholia.

It was that very afternoon that I came home to find Mr and Mrs Williams, Manda's parents, in the kitchen talking to Mum and Dad. They broke off rather suddenly when I walked in through the back door, so I realised they were not just paying a social call.

'She can't go to her Aunty Beth's,' I heard Mrs Williams say, as I went on up the stairs, 'because she's having a baby and frankly we'd rather she and Mary weren't under the same roof.' I could not think what she was talking about, until I remembered that Mary Jenkins was now living with her father, Dr Davidson, who had married Manda's Aunt Beth last summer. But why couldn't Manda stay at *home*? If it had been anyone else they had been talking about, I would not have been remotely interested, but anything to do with Manda seemed to absorb my entire being.

Later that evening the mystery was solved, when Mum and Dad, (rather diffidently, I thought) asked me if I would mind if Manda came to live with us for a while. I was practically struck dumb. We must have had hundreds of people staying with us during my life, but they had never before asked if I *minded*.

'Why?' I asked to cover my surprise.

'Her father was transferred to his firm's Manchester branch a few months back, and he just comes home at weekends. But that's being rather a strain all round, and now they've got an excellent offer for their house her mother feels she should go up and join him. But Manda wants to stay in Fleetbridge until her exams are over.' I knew that was not the only reason she wanted to get away from her mother, but I did not say so because the thought of having Manda *living* in our house was making me giddy.

'Wherever will she sleep?' was all I said.

'Joyce and Sue and the babies are going to share a flat from next week,' said Mum, 'so she can have their room.'

I had not forgotten the cockadoodledoo remark, so I growled 'Good riddance, at least Manda won't scream half the night.'

She came in early December, but it felt more like May time to me. She had the capacity to make everyone happy around her, even George had a bath!

'I can't think of anywhere I'd rather live than here,' she said one day as she beamed round the supper table. I said she must be mad, but she certainly looked a lot less strained without her mother fussing over every minute of her life. She was also looking stronger, but I doubted if she would fatten up much on Mum's cooking.

The house seemed even more crowded than ever after Manda came. People were always popping in to see her, and drinking endless cups of coffee in our kitchen. The whole house seemed full of laughter, and I began to grudge the hours I had to spend *away* from it. I did manage to fit in those guitar lessons, and they were pure joy, but I had a sneaking feeling that Manda did not really need them, she was becoming very good without any help from me.

'What a ministry of song God has given her.' I guessed the old ladies were saying that in church about Manda now.

But I think she really made the most difference to Kevin's life. He took to her in the most amazing way. She fed him, pushed him out for walks in his wheelchair and talked to him endlessly – just as if he was an ordinary boy of sixteen.

'You've got a real gift with handicapped people,' said

Kevin's mother, Joan, one evening. 'He's never let anyone else feed him but me.'

'Perhaps he knows I'm handicapped too,' replied Manda softly, and she looked at him so lovingly I felt ridiculously jealous.

Chapter Twelve

Zac's Surprise

I had a really dirty cold on the fateful night we went to Catford.

'Why don't you stay at home tonight, Davy,' fussed Mum. 'It's so foggy and cold out.'

I was sorely tempted, until I discovered that Manda was going out to a church social.

My lofty seat on top of the speakers felt even more uncomfortable than usual as we hurtled towards London, every bone in my body ached and my throat felt as if I'd swallowed a pint of acid.

The only drop of comfort I had was the fact that Steve also had my cold, and he hadn't even turned out! A gig without Steve might prove quite a pleasant experience, but later that night I was to long for his karate chop and even Devil's sharp teeth.

When we reached our destination, we found ourselves in a very rough area indeed, and the Youth Club where we were booked was a punk stronghold. (Another drop of comfort – no curly wig!) We were standing in for a punk rock band or we would never have been offered the gig. There was too much competition in London; Brighton was the usual ceiling of our ambition.

They were a great audience, and they really loved me – I would have enjoyed myself hugely if I hadn't sounded like a rook in a church belfry. We might have got away with it if they had liked the sketches, but drama just did not switch them on. They wanted music, and Trev's drumming drove them crazy with delight.

I was just trying out my latest song called 'Satan the ruler of the world' when the first disaster struck. Simon was supposed to let off several chemical smoke bombs which were to curl round our knees and add to the sinister flavour of the number. But the wally overdid it and reduced my already dicy respiratory system to a coughing, sneezing standstill. I shot Zac a desperate look through the dense smoke. Without Steve, there was nothing for it but to get Joe to do the vocal lead.

He could hardly speak because of his terrible stutter, but strangely he could sing even if he did sound like the braying of an agitated donkey! He shambled through life in a world of his own, looking like a gangling telegraph pole with arms and legs screwed on too loosely; but that audience must have been tone deaf. Anyway they loved him, and all the girls swarmed round him at the end of every number, patting his hair and asking him questions about his personal life.

I could never fathom why girls always did that to Joe, and when he didn't answer they thought he was the strong silent type and never guessed he was too scared to speak in case he stuttered.

We were beginning to run out of our heavy rock numbers, and even Trev was slowing down when the shabby doors at the back of the hall crashed open and with wild war cries a rival gang of mods burst in for a full-scale smash up.

Our punk audience lost all interest in us, and turned in fury to defend their territory.

'Take our stuff, and get out of here,' shouted Zac urgently, but he was too late. The mods saw my hairdo and thinking we were the enemy, they swarmed on to the stage.

'This is your fault for being a punk,' screamed Monkey, and at that moment I really longed for my wretched blond wig, not to mention Steve and Devil.

I have a fleeting memory of Simon jumping up and down in impotent agitation while three of them kicked to death his best speaker, and Trev disappearing off the stage clutching his precious bass drum like an outsized baby. After that my recollections are hazy as huge fists exploded at me from all directions.

I can just remember the police whistles, and the siren of the ambulance that took me away.

'You are mostly in one piece,' grinned an Indian doctor, endless hours later. 'Just a few bruises and bangs, but you do seem to have broken your nose. I'll just get a nurse to pack it.' I had seen this film before, and I groaned.

It was two days later and I was on my way down to supper. Two navy blue eyes gazed back balefully at me as I passed my old friend the mirror. Why had I been born with a nose that stuck out so far it was a positive danger to itself? But at least the plaster hid some of the acne.

I had been in bed for the last two days licking my wounds, but I really had to get myself round to the stables that evening. We had such a huge load of bookings over the Christmas holiday that every minute of rehearsal time was vital.

I eased my bruises down beside Manda and mentally murdered Pam for giggling at my grotesque appearance.

Mum was just starting to dish up the curry when there was a ring at the doorbell. That happens so often at the Manse, that it hardly registered. But I nearly shot out of my seat when I heard Zac's voice in the hall. I had deliberately kept him away from my home, ashamed of its shabby appearance and odd inhabitants, and I was not sure if Mum and Dad would approve of him.

'Come right in,' said Mum giving her universal welcome.

'I just came to ask how David is. My name's Zac.' Dad shot up from the table and out into the hall.

'Come on in, and have some tea with us,' he said as if Zac had been the Prime Minister. 'We've been longing to meet you.'

It was not a Kevin night, and that, coupled with the fact that George was safely in hospital having his bunions fixed, caused me as much relief as Dad's reaction. But I still sat there willing John not to burp. There was an empty place next to Dad, and he and Zac were soon talking away as if they had known each other for years. Dad has a way of making people relax and talk about themselves. I suppose it's his job really, but I could see Zac liked him.

He and Dad went on talking while the rest of us washed up and were still at it when people began to drift off to different parts of the house. Zac is what my old Gran would have called 'a gentleman', which really means he can charm older people until he gets them eating out of his hand.

My nose was hurting, and I knew I'd never get through an evening in the stables without a couple of the painkillers the hospital had given me, so I went upstairs to fetch them feeling cross. I was two different people; but I did not want Dad or Zac to realise that, which was the real reason I had tried to keep them apart.

It was when I was on my way down that I froze on the stairs. They were talking about me. I crept a little nearer to the open kitchen door telling myself I had a right to know what they were saying.

'How good is David, Zac?' Dad was saying. 'Musically I mean.'

'Well he's certainly improved our sound,' laughed Zac,

'and he's brought in his own brand of humour – it's making us much more commercial than we were. People like laughing. It's very rare as well, to get a lead singer who plays the guitar well too, usually they only strum.'

'But is he good enough to make it in the pop world?' persisted Dad. 'Do it as a career I mean.' There was a long pause and when Zac spoke again he sounded embarrassed.

'He'd never make it on his own in an ordinary band,' he replied at last. 'His looks are against him, but that wouldn't matter so much if he had a big personality, but . . . perhaps he and I might have a future together in films or TV.'

Dad laughed, 'That's not an easy world to get into.' 'But it would be for me,' replied Zac. 'You see my father has masses of contacts. In a few years time when we've worked on our technique, he'll pull all the strings for us.'

I lowered my bruised body down on to the bottom step of the stairs. No looks, no personality. Was I going to have to depend on Zac for ever, or even worse, be his father's parasite?

Then I heard Zac ask a very strange question. 'Do you mind Davo messing about with us? I mean it's not your scene is it?'

Annoyance flooded through me masking the hurt I had been feeling before. They were discussing me as if I had been a child.

'I don't think I would mind if I thought he was really happy,' said Dad slowly, 'but I don't really think he is. Are *you* happy Zac?'

'Happy!' replied Zac with a bitter edge to his voice. 'What's happy? I do everything I do just to keep myself from going under.'

'Under to what?' asked Dad gently.

'Under to . . . well it's like I'm standing on the edge of a precipice and looking down there's a great boiling steaming black hole. One skid in the wrong direction, and I'm down in it.' I felt Dad was sure to start telling him about Jesus, and I just could not bear it, so I bounced back into the room making as much noise as possible.

'David,' said Dad, as I gulped down my pills, 'Zac reminds me of someone, but I can't think who it is.'

'I always think that,' I said, trying not to scowl – it made my face hurt too much.

'It'll probably come to me one day when I'm preaching,' laughed Dad, and then becoming suddenly serious he said, 'Zac, how would it be if you and your group came and played to our youth group's Christmas party, it's on the eighteenth.'

'Dad!' I protested, 'we're Anarchists!' Whatever would happen if Zac put on some of his cruder sketches. I'd probably die of embarrassment, and my latest song about Satan would hardly go down with that audience.

'We'll come,' said Zac unexpectedly. 'The eighteenth is about the only free evening we've got in weeks.'

'Come on Zac,' I said sourly, 'we're late already, the others'll be fuming at the stable.'

He was oddly quiet as we walked down the road. Suddenly he astonished me by saying, 'You know what Davo, I'd give my Sunday best eyeballs for a home like yours.'

'Like mine?' I exploded, stopping dead in the middle of the pavement. 'But you've got all the things you could possibly want, clothes, money – everything. Do you realise just how poor we are?'

'What does that matter,' snapped Zac. 'My Dad only pays me to keep out of his way – your parents really care about *you*.'

'Care about ME! They couldn't care less.'

'That's just where you're wrong, Davo,' said Zac with

conviction. 'I can't ever remember meeting such great people. I may have got a lot of *things*, but I've got no *people* at all.'

'Well, I've always had far *too many* people,' I spluttered, 'and I can't wait to get *things*, big expensive, extravagant *things*. Who needs people?'

'Sometimes Davo,' said Zac kicking open the stable door, 'you're an even bigger fool than you look, and that's saying something.'

'You've got to be out of your crazy little mind!' exploded Steve, and Devil snarled his agreement. 'Play in a church? What'll our following think of us?'

'It's not a church,' replied Zac impatiently, 'it's a hall.'

'They won't pay us,' said Monkey knowingly.

'Well, Christmas is for charity, isn't it?' demanded Zac.

'You won't catch me in a goys church,' added Monkey, standing on his head.

'Thought you weren't orthodox,' growled Zac, opening a new bottle of vodka.

'I'm not,' said Monkey, his upside down face splitting into a sudden grin, 'but I can't let myself sink that low.'

'Nor can I,' said Steve unpleasantly.

'Are you a Jew too?' sneered Zac.

'No,' replied Steve grandly. 'I'm a Satanist – sold my soul to the devil last term when Mary was at school.' I shivered. Was he joking or just trying to shock us? He couldn't be serious, or could he? I'd had enough of that kind of thing for one lifetime.

'I used to go to Sunday school there,' said Trev suddenly. 'They sing this song. It goes "red and yellow, black and white all are precious in His sight," then the kids all laughed at me 'cos I'm black. There weren't no reds or yellows there, so I left.'

'What's that got to do with it,' snapped Zac. He was not

100

used to insubordination, and I'd never seen him so angry. When Joe actually managed to stutter, 'I wwwwwwwwouldn't be seen dead in a chchchchchchurch,' Zac finally lost his cool.

'Look, you horrible little lot,' he blazed slamming his fists down on the bar. 'I've said we're going and we *are* going. Even if I have to do my solo impersonations. But I'm telling you straight, if you don't all show that night, this outfit's over.'

'What d'you mean?' demanded Steve leaning menacingly over the bar towards Zac.

'This is my place,' hissed Zac, 'every bit of gear we use was paid for by my Dad, and you're all such fools you couldn't begin to operate unless I showed you how.'

'Just 'cos you're a filthy rich poser, doesn't mean you own us,' said Steve in a dangerously quiet voice.

'But I *do* own you,' smiled Zac contemptuously, 'and if you don't do as I say, I'll do without you.'

There was a long silence. Steve flexed his karate hand, while the rest of us held our breath knowing this clash had been brewing for months.

'We'll play it your way *this* time,' growled Steve sullenly, but there was something about the way he looked at Zac that made me fear he'd pay for his victory, and once again I shivered. Yes, I was frightened of Steve.

Chapter Thirteen

Jesus, Where Are You?

I had felt apprehensive all day, and even the Christmas festivities of the last day of term had not cheered my gloom. I did not want to look into the faces of the youth group and sing to them again, and what if Steve and the others messed everything up and made me look a fool? I wanted to keep my two worlds as far apart as possible. But it was not just that. As I walked home through the biting sleet, I realised why I felt so miserable. I was missing God. 'I must believe in Him,' I thought, 'or I would not mind so much.' I really felt as if I was in mourning for someone I'd loved all my life. Going back to youth group would be like visiting a graveyard.

Of course, it wasn't like an ordinary Friday evening. Because it was the Christmas party, there were piles of gorgeous eats, and all the girls were togged up in full regalia. But there was only one girl in the hall I cared about, and she hardly noticed I was there. Dan was expected home from College at any moment, and she could hardly wrench her eyes from the doors at the back of the hall.

Zac possessed the great gift of being able instinctively to judge the taste of his audience. We never churned out the same old programme, but he adapted like a chameleon to our surroundings. Zac had put together three sets that evening that would have satisfied a parcel of Bishops.

'None of your blue jokes,' he hissed to Monkey just before the first sketch.

'You're lucky I'm here at all,' spat Monkey. 'If my Dad knew, he'd kill me.'

Tess was wearing her bored look and Trev registered his protest by playing his drums with his back to the audience. I could not help noticing that Michelle looked thin and strained under all her make-up. She was hopelessly in love with Steve, who never looked beyond Tess.

Zac had written some hilarious sketches for our Christmas gigs and with the cruder scenes left out, we soon had our audience cracking up. Dad sat at the back and positively cried laughing at Father Christmas getting helplessly stuck in the chimney, not to mention Monkey as a Christmas tree fairy. Simon had invented some flashing tree lights that he stuck on my skull at the base of my green fringe, and with that and my 'twinkling' red nose, I was the recurring gag of the evening. But I felt like the clown with the broken heart when Dan finally showed up, and Manda positively fell into his arms.

'There's something odd about this lot,' remarked Zac with his mouth full of mince pie. We were taking a break before our finale and the Youth Group were clustering round us as we sat on the edge of the stage. The rest of the Anarchists, who were still very hostile had nipped round to the pub for a drink.

'What do you mean odd?' I asked sharply. I didn't mind thinking they were all fools, but I wasn't going to have anyone else saying so.

'Hang about,' he soothed, 'they're the best audience we ever had. It's just that it's hard to believe they can be that happy only on coke. I've never met people like this before.'

'Have another mince pie,' said Dad coming up to us with a plateful. I could see they were Mum's because they were all burnt – hers always get left to last.

'This lot don't seem to have any problems,' said Zac wistfully looking round the hall.

'God takes them all away,' I said cynically.

'He doesn't!' laughed Dad, looking at Rosey, Pam and John. 'Everyone has problems, it's what we do with them that counts.'

'What can you do with problems, except escape from them?' said Zac wearily.

'Sometimes you can't escape,' said Dad, watching Manda shuffling across the room. 'But you can let them make you bitter or better.' Zac stood and looked at Dad for a long time and then with a shrug he turned away.

I always feel terrible just before I sing one of my own songs for the first time. You share a small snippet of your soul with the audience, and if they don't like it, you feel personally rejected. A few days before, Zac had said, 'Davo, why not write a carol to round off our Christmas set – a bit of religion sometimes goes down quite well at Christmas.' Now as I adjusted my plectrum and waited for Trev's intro, I cursed Zac for making me christen it here. I had poured too much of my own longings and despair into the lyrics. What would Dad think of it?

> *Oh Jesus, Jesus where have you gone?*
> *Why are you hiding from me?*

The first line fell into the silent hall like a pebble into a deep pool. It was strange to be listened to again. I felt a right wally singing those words in my fairy lights, but strangely I think they added to the pathos.

> *I looked for you inside the church,*
>   *but they told me to wipe my feet.*
> *I looked for you inside my school*
>   *but they told me to cut my hair.*
> *I looked for you in a busy street*
>   *but the people pushed me aside.*

104

> *So I walked into a refugee camp*
> *but I couldn't see you there.*
> *And then I saw a dying child lying in the dirt*
> *Oh Jesus, Jesus where were you then*
> *Why didn't you feel his hurt?*
> *You were born as a refugee*
> *and nobody cared for you.*
> *So why did you leave that child to die?*
> *Don't you care that I'm searching for you?*

Every other item we had done that evening had been met by thunderous applause, but the silence that greeted my carol was uncanny. Dad jumped on to the stage to cover the awkwardness and thank us all for coming, but I could see he had tears in his eyes. Why couldn't he tell me right out what he thought of my song?

'Told you all that religious stuff would be enough to flatten any audience,' grumbled Steve, as we began to dismantle the gear.

'It wasn't that they didn't like it,' said Zac thoughtfully. He was standing in the middle of the stage getting in everyone's way. 'It made them sad. I think they miss you Davo.'

'Don't be a twit,' I snapped. 'They're glad to be rid of me.'

Girls were swarming round Joe and Steve, while the boys chatted up Tess. The world streamed on round Zac, and I jumped off the stage to coil up the speaker wires. It was then that I noticed Dan. Something was very wrong with him.

Manda was talking, laughing and sparkling up at him, but he stood like an unresponsive lamppost, and gradually her sparkle was dying away.

When I had waved the van off down the road, I went into

the Manse and found Dan in the kitchen while Mum tried to make him finish up her burnt mince pies. We could all see he was not his usual bouncy self, and Dad gave us all a firm wink, and we tactfully melted away and left the two of them alone with the mince pies.

'Early night will do us all good,' giggled Pam, but I went into the sitting room muttering about a TV programme I wanted to see. 'Sitting room' is a stupid name, no one ever 'sits' in there. There was nothing I wanted to watch, of course, I just wanted to be near to Manda.

I couldn't think what time it was. I must have fallen asleep on the floor. The telly screen was blank, and it must have been the front door shutting behind Dan that had woken me up. I scooped myself up stiffly from the floor and staggered into the kitchen, a nice bowl of cornflakes floating in my imagination. Then I saw Manda. She was crumpled over the table with her head resting on the crook of her arm and she was crying in a way that I find painful to remember.

I never had a sister or a girlfriend, and Mum never cries, so I simply did not know what to do. So I collected a bunch of kitchen paper and sat down awkwardly beside her. I didn't think she knew I was even there until she suddenly said, 'I knew this was going to happen.'

'Want to talk about it?' I said, sounding like an American TV programme. She looked at me with dull, heavy eyes. 'No,' she said. End of conversation. Dad would handle this much better. I wondered if I should run up and wake him.

'You're well rid of him,' I said hopefully.

'I'm not!' she said crossly. 'I can't think how I'll live without him. But I knew it would happen. Someone as gorgeous as Dan would never want to stay tied down to a smashed up freak of a schoolgirl.'

'You're not a smashed up freak!' I said passionately.

'You're the most wonderful person I've ever known,' but I doubt if she even heard me. So I muttered, 'Found someone else has he?'

'He didn't say so,' she sniffed, 'but I could see by his eyes that he doesn't love me any more. So I told him to push off. I don't want his pity, and I don't want yours,' she added furiously, 'so you can stop looking at me like that, David.'

'I'm not looking like anything,' I said hurriedly. 'You ought to have a cup of tea with lots of sugar in it,' I added remembering my cub scout first aid badge.

'I hate tea,' said Manda furiously, and the conversation died again.

'It's good really I suppose,' she continued as she shredded the kitchen paper like a gerbil. 'I think I've been relying on him too much. When I was at Stoke Mandeville, I was always doubting God and letting things get me down, but then Dan'd come up for the weekend and I'd be all right again. I think I've been worshipping God *through* him really. The other day in church, I felt God saying to me that He wanted me to rely just on Him. But I . . .' Suddenly she dissolved into tears again, and to my amazement she put her head down on my shoulder. I suppose it wouldn't have mattered to her whose shoulder it was, anyone's would have done. But I had dreamed for months of something like this happening, but in my imagination she had not been crying for someone else's love, nothing ever goes quite right for me. It is truly amazing that girls can cry that much and not dehydrate.

Of course I had to bungle the first love scene of my life. I played it all wrong. Zac would have been ashamed of me. 'Manda,' I said in a sickly voice, 'I've loved you for months, couldn't we . . . I mean . . .' She sat up and slid away from me along the bench. Would she laugh at me – make a joke about my nose or spots? Tess would have done.

'Thank you David,' she said in a small voice. 'That's nice of you.' Glorious hope hit me like a punch in the back of my jeans. 'Then could we . . . ?'

'No David,' she replied gently. 'You'd pull me away from God. One day I just might learn to live without Dan, but no way could I possibly cope without God. Life's so ghastly now I can't really walk. He's the only reason I've got for going on living.'

'You might pull me in His direction,' I said hopefully.

'No I wouldn't,' she said. 'I know I'm just not strong enough.' Fumbling for her stick, she groped her way blindly towards the door. 'David,' she said, as she turned the old-fashioned handle, 'that new song of yours – you've got God wrong.' She stood with her back up against the kitchen door, and tried so hard to twist her face into a smile. 'You told me once you'd outgrown God, but you've never even known Him.'

'I've lived with Him in this house all my life,' I protested.

'Then why can't you see how much He cares for people who are hurting and being smashed about? It breaks His heart when people don't understand how much He longs to help them.'

'But look at you,' I almost shouted. 'You're having a job just to stand up there. Don't you blame Him for that?'

'I'm happier now than I ever was before I knew Him,' she replied simply. 'Happiness doesn't depend on what you can do, or what you have, it's how you feel inside that counts.' Then she was gone, and I was left staring at the blank kitchen door.

When I got in from my paper round next morning, she had gone home to Manchester, and the Manse felt desolate in spite of the Christmas tree.

Chapter Fourteen

Tragedy

It was a shining, frosty night towards the end of January, and Christmas and the New Year were just an exhausting memory. Playing at a different party every night for a month may sound exciting, but really it was just plain boring, and I would have given anything just to stay at home with a good book. The only thing that kept me from going under with sheer exhaustion, was the happy feeling that we were making a lot of money at last, but I soon blew my share on clothes at the January sales.

The festive season was quietening down a bit now, but the gigs were still coming in thick and fast because I think we were changing our style, producing a more commercial sound, and the sketches were less serious and more entertaining.

I looked across the supper table at Manda. She had come back after Christmas her usual smiley self. It was only when she thought people weren't watching her, that she gave herself away and allowed her mouth to droop down at the corners. She was feeding Kevin while he lovingly patted her arm. I could feel Dad watching me in much the same anxious way I was watching Manda.

I willed myself not to meet his eyes up the table. He was looking thinner and older suddenly, and I knew he was not sleeping well. He always seemed to be up, prowling round the house whatever time I got in. Something was worrying him.

'Manda,' I said suddenly, attempting to shut Dad out of my mind, 'what are you doing tonight?'

'Homework I suppose,' she answered with a sigh.

'Why not come round to the stable, and give us a hand painting some scenery?' I adored the way her nose wrinkled up when she smiled.

'All right,' she said, 'I've always wanted to see what you all do in that place.'

'She couldn't walk that far,' fussed Mum.

'I'll push her in the wheelchair then.' Manda grumbled about that, but I got her into it in the end, and packed her well round with rugs and a couple of extra scarves. 'I won't come at all if you keep on like an old hen,' she protested. But soon we were gliding away over the icy pavements, under the romantic stars. I've never known anyone who was such fun to be with as Manda.

We were just steaming up the hill over the common, when suddenly, from the road on our right leapt a motorbike. Its headlight dazzled us as it took the corner with a screech of brakes. Manda screamed and tried to jump out of the wheelchair. Her legs tangled in the rugs and she fell into the frosted grass by the path. 'He must have been a madman!' she gasped furiously.

'No,' I laughed, when I was sure she was not hurt. 'That was only Joe on his new bike.'

'He ought to be prosecuted,' she said crossly, as I hauled her back into the chair.

'But it's the best thing that ever happened to him,' I protested. 'He's been saving up for years and he's been a new man since he got it.'

Manda's sense of humour trickled slowly back. 'You see, I've had this recurring nightmare, since the accident,' she explained with a sheepish giggle. 'These lights come out of the darkness at me, and I hear this awful scream . . .' We went on towards Zac's place, but somehow the magic of the evening had faded, and I was beginning to wish I had not brought her. Zac didn't like strangers sitting in on our rehearsals, and Steve was always so unpleasant to Manda at school. Suppose he started on her tonight?

But I need not have worried. As soon as I pushed her into the warmth and brilliant light of the stable, Zac leapt down from the stage and bounded over towards us. 'You're just the person I wanted to see,' he said, helping her out of the chair and drawing her over towards the bar. I realised that he was always strangely warm towards anyone from the Manse, and as the others usually took their cue from him, I sighed with relief.

Zac pushed Joe off the bar stool where he was sitting, still wearing his crash helmet and swigging gin like a baby swallows its milk.

'Perch yourself on this,' smiled Zac, 'and I'll get you a drink. What are you having?'

'Coke?' asked Manda shyly.

'Coke!' laughed Zac. 'Don't be a baby, have some vodka.'

'No thanks,' said Manda firmly. 'I'll have some orange or something.'

'Come on,' bullied Zac, his face clouding. He hated people who would not drink with him. But Manda laughingly insisted on her orange juice. 'In Stoke I saw so many people who had their lives smashed because they drank too much, it's put me off the stuff for life.'

'I admire you for that,' said Zac suddenly. 'I'm hooked on it myself, but I would give anything to be free. But, look, we need your help,' he continued changing the subject suddenly. 'Davo tells me you sing your own songs.' He was leaning on the bar, smiling down at her, and if he hadn't been my best friend I would have hated him.

'My Dad's got a client who's running a charity dinner in

Brighton. It's in aid of physically handicapped children. We've got to entertain all these toffee-nosed people and make them part with their money. Until you came through that door I honestly didn't know how we could do it. If you sat in the wheelchair and sang to them, we'd have them crying all the way to the bank.'

'All right,' laughed Manda, 'and I'll put white powder on my face and make myself look half dead if you like.'

'Shouldn't bother with the make-up,' said Tess spitefully, 'it's not necessary.' But I don't think Manda heard her.

She ran through three of her songs and she sounded so good I felt fiercely proud of her; but I became increasingly aware of Tess, biting the air viciously, and positively seething with rage. Steve was standing with his arm round Tess's quivering shoulders, and suddenly I was afraid.

'God, God, God, God, God!' exploded Steve when Manda's voice finally died away. 'That's all we ever get these days. We had to put up with Concorde wally's carol for weeks and now this.'

'That carol was very popular,' said Zac mildly.

'Well, people don't mind that kind of stuff at Christmas, but you can't force another starry-eyed angel on us.' There was an uncomfortable silence, while Joe had another gin and Monkey stood on his head. Manda looked from Tess to Steve and laughed. 'Don't get eggy,' she said, 'I've got exams to pass. I'm already a year behind. I haven't really got time to be a starry-eyed angel, but I will sing with you this time, because it's a good cause.'

'Good cause!' sneered Steve. 'Handicapped people ought to be put down like sick animals.' I was so horrified I felt as if someone was choking me. Zac's face wore a strange expression, but it was Monkey who acted first.

'That's what Hitler thought!' he said swinging himself upright.

112

'Good for him,' growled Steve. 'Who wants spastics and Jews anyway.' The shock waves travelled round the stables leaving us all speechless. Joe cowered behind the bar clutching his bottle of gin; Trev's eyes rolled white with emotion in his black face; and even Simon took his head out of his electronics catalogue and peered at us through his thick glasses.

I've often wondered what would have happened if, just at that very minute both halves of the stable door had not burst open, and there stood Zac's father. In all the months I'd been coming to the stable, I had never seen him before. He was a bloated, distorted version of Zac. In his hand he waved a piece of paper. He was drunk and extremely angry.

'Look at this!' he shouted advancing towards the bar. 'You'll have to bring your own drink in. Why should I pay bills like this?' He thrust his puffy, florid face at Joe and glared in at him through the visor of his helmet. 'I'm going to start charging you rent for this place,' he added nastily, 'and if there's one thing I hate, it's motorbikes.'

'And if there's one thing I hate, it's you,' breathed Zac when his father had slammed the doors behind him. Suddenly I realised that the suave, self-confident Zac I knew, looked like a frightened little boy when his father was around. An odd feeling of envy hit me. Life would have been easier for me if I could have hated my father, I would not have felt so bad about myself. It's hard work living with saints.

'I think we'd better go home, David,' whispered Manda, but Monkey had grabbed his jacket and was out of the doors before us.

I pushed the wheelchair into the yard, and Manda was just climbing in as Joe revved up his engine noisily.

'Don't do that!' hissed Zac. 'Dad's in a horrible mood these days.'

'You ought to leave that thing here and walk,' said Trev. 'You've had so much gin you couldn't ride a kiddie's tricycle.' But Joe only grinned at us through his plastic window, and shot away spraying us all with gravel from the drive. We never saw him again. Two minutes later he hit a patch of ice and that was that.

When I got home for breakfast on Friday, Dad was reading the local paper.

'This lad Joe Lee, who was killed on his motorbike. Wasn't he in your group?' he asked.

'He played keyboard,' I answered dully, gazing stupidly at my plate of bacon and eggs. The news of his death had broken over us four days before, but I was still in a state of shock.

'It says here that he'd been drinking,' continued Dad miserably. Zac's white face seemed to stare back at me from my greasy plate. 'I should never have let him go with a skinful like that,' Zac had said that over and over again like a gramophone record. 'It's our fault he's dead.'

The local paper suddenly collapsed like the walls of Jericho and Dad's anxious face peered at me from where it had been.

'Davy, who drives that great van you all go round in?' I knew what he was getting at, and I poked my cold egg defensively. None of us was safe when Big Jim had quenched his massive thirst. But I wasn't going to have Dad jaw me about the evils of drink, so I filled my mouth too full of bacon to speak. But all Dad said was, 'Be careful won't you? You're so precious to us.' I looked right into his face, and suddenly I believed him. Mum was up the business end of the kitchen burning the toast, and no one else was down yet. Suddenly the wall that I had been building between me and Dad began to crumble. I yearned

114

to tell him just how Joe's death had made me feel —
uncertain — terrified of the blackness that lay at the far end
of a life without God, but somehow I couldn't seem to
swallow that wretched bacon.

'Sometimes,' said Dad gently, 'we long for freedom to do
as we like, but then we find we don't really like what we
do.' He had hit my nail so perfectly on its head, that I
choked on the bacon. The 'phone rang, Pam and John
clattered into the room and my chance was gone. The
moment was lost for ever.

Chapter Fifteen

Troubles for Zac

Zac and I stared at one another over the stained table in the pub. I knew that the stark horror I could see in his eyes were mirrored in my own.

'That was ghastly,' he said as he downed his second double whisky.

Joe had said he wouldn't be seen dead in a church, but he'd had no option that morning when the old Fleetbridge Parish Church had been thronged with people who had never even noticed him when he lived. All the Anarchists had been given a morning off to go to the funeral, and Tess had cried so much for the boy she'd always despised, that her face was streaked with mascara, and Monkey had whispered as we stood by the grave, 'You goys just don't know how to run funerals.' They had all gone back to school with Miss Carmichael and Mr Atkins, but Zac had muttered, 'I need a drink,' and we melted into the crowd, rammed our blazers and ties into our bags and made for the nearest pub. He looked so green, I was worried about him.

'The worst bit was when Martin walked in behind the coffin.' I shuddered. 'It was just as if Joe had come back with clean clothes and a haircut — it must be terrible to have a twin brother die.'

Zac looked up at me sharply. 'Some things are worse than dying,' he said in a strange voice.

'Like what?' I demanded with a shiver.

'Living,' said Zac wearily.

I pretended I had not heard him, and said, 'I've always wished I had a twin brother, used to pretend I had when I was little.'

'You might not have liked it so much if you had one,' he said bitterly, and he pushed back his chair abruptly and went off to get us more drinks.

'You said you were going dry, when you heard about Joe,' I reminded him when he came back.

'I can't,' he said hopelessly. I was feeling thoroughly uneasy. I must snap him out of this mood, the whole thing had upset him too much.

'What's so bad about living?' I said bracingly. 'We'll soon be making so much money we can really enjoy ourselves.'

'My Dad's *made* lots of money, and he's about the most miserable specimen I know,' growled Zac.

'Well, his wife's left him,' I said, and Zac laughed in my face. 'He was even more miserable before she did. Everything seems so pointless,' he added bleakly. 'I used to think we could do something worthwhile with the sketches, but people will only pay us to make them laugh, not to make them think. They don't care about anything that's real. We're all just trying to escape from life, that's all. Joe's the lucky one, he's managed it.' We sat on until closing time. He'd be better in a few days, I told myself, but if I had known what was going to happen that night, I would have been even more worried than I was.

We got together that evening at the stable, more for mutual support than a workout. They tried to run through some of the sketches that might have been suitable for the Charity Dinner, but no one really had the heart to be creative and Monkey and Trev still weren't talking to Steve so the atmosphere was somewhat strained. The fact that the bar was as bare as Old Mother Hubbard's cupboard, did

117

nothing to lift the gloom. I had refused to bring Manda again. She'd have to sing on Saturday without a backing from us. I could just about stand Steve slanging *me*, but no way was I going to expose Manda to his brutality.

Zac was as tense as a tightrope that night. Something was happening over at the house. The yard and drive were positively littered with huge, expensive cars and lights gleamed from the mullioned windows.

'Your Dad havin' a party?' asked Steve, leaning like a thirsty horse over the stable door.

'Can't be having much fun,' added Tess curiously, 'they're not making a sound.'

'Come away from there!' ordered Zac urgently. 'Dad said you weren't to be here tonight – something nasty's going on – I don't like it.'

'We'd better go then,' said Steve nervously. 'If we go now the pubs'll still be open.'

'Don't go, Davo,' said Zac as I was about to follow them out of the door. No one had ever wanted my company before, and the appeal in his frightened dark eyes was unmistakable. He switched off the lights, and we sat waiting in the silence. I had no idea what we were waiting for, but I sensed danger all round us, and I would have given anything to run home to the safety, laughter and warmth of the Manse, but for some reason Zac needed me, so I stayed.

The day had been so traumatic, that I think I must have dozed off with my back against the stage. Anyway the police whistle practically sent me six feet into the air. Zac and I both dived for the stable door just in time to see dark figures detach themselves from the shadows of the garden and yard, springing towards the house. Suddenly, the ominous silence erupted into noisy confusion. Doors banged, men shouted and a woman screamed. I definitely heard several gun shots followed by an explosion of breaking glass. The house was now completely surrounded by scores of policemen and their dogs, and I felt sick with horror when I saw men with rifles breaking their way into the back door. We shut ourselves in and crouched behind the bar. I could not see Zac in the darkness, but I felt his whole body shaking, and I was nearly deafened by my own heartbeats.

The noise and confusion outside seemed to reach a frenzied climax, then heavy feet crunched on the gravel of the drive and car doors banged in the road beyond the garden.

'The pigs are taking them away,' hissed Zac as he stumbled over to the door again. We were just in time to see his father hustled out of the house by two policemen, followed by the woman who was not his wife. They were handcuffed and their faces looked ghastly in the moonlight.

'Dad!' screamed Zac, 'What's happening?' A huge bulky sergeant brought him down with a rugger tackle.

'Get off!' shouted Zac's father, 'He doesn't know anything about this, he's only a kid.' The policeman pulled himself wheezing to his feet, and suddenly he looked sickeningly familiar.

'Where's your Mum, lad?' he asked as Zac's father was hurried away into the darkness.

'She went years ago,' muttered Zac.

'We'll take you to her,' said the sergeant seizing Zac by the arm and trying to drag him down the drive as well.

'No way!' said Zac vehemently. 'I'm staying here, *this* is my home.'

'Sorry lad,' said the sergeant, 'but we have to search this place and then close it up for security reasons. Haven't you got any other relations?'

'You've just arrested the only one I've got,' said Zac dully. 'I haven't got anywhere to go.'

'Then I'm afraid you'll have to come with me, and we'll sort something out down at the station.'

'You're not dragging me off in one of your pig vans!' shouted Zac wildly. 'I haven't done anything!'

I did not want to meet that sergeant again face to face, but I really could not leave Zac in the middle of an earthquake like that, so I stepped out of the darkness of the stable. Two sweating constables grabbed me at once, forcing my arms behind my back. Someone shone a powerful torch into my face and I heard the sergeant's grunt of recognition.

'He could come to our house,' I squeaked nervously. 'My Mum and Dad wouldn't mind.'

'You're Mr Martin the minister's son,' stated the sergeant smugly. 'Very fine man *he* is.' I felt he wanted to add, 'which is more than can be said for his son', but he managed not to. 'We'll take you round there and see if he'll put you up, anyway for the night,' he wheezed, 'but first we'd better take you up to pack a few things. You won't be coming back here for a while, lad.'

Mum saw the police car draw up at the gate from her bedroom window, and she opened the door to us in her dressing gown and hair rollers. 'What's he done *this* time?' she gasped when she saw the policeman standing behind me.

Before anyone could answer her, Zac crumpled like a limp rag doll at her feet. I suppose the horrors of the day had just been too much for him. The sergeant took a deep breath and began his explanations, but no one stopped to listen. Dad and John padded downstairs in their slippers, and together they lifted Zac into the kitchen and sat him by the Aga with his head between his knees.

Mum is always at her best in a crisis, and she soon had Pam making up a bed in my room, while she and Manda flapped round filling hot-water bottles and making endless cups of tea. I nearly cracked up when Dad went to the first aid box and measured out a couple of teaspoons of whisky. I didn't like to tell him that it would have taken an awful lot more than that to pull Zac round!

It felt as if the tide had gone out after a great storm when finally the police had gone. Zac was settled in bed, the light was out and the house was quiet at last. I thought he'd fallen alseep, but suddenly I heard his muffled voice through the safe cosy darkness of my attic. 'There's nowhere in all the world I would rather be than here,' he said. 'I feel safe in this house. Your Mum and Dad . . .' His voice trailed sleepily away, but as I lay there I realised for the first time just what our home must have felt like to John when he had first crawled through the door, or Pam, covered in bruises, Kevin's mum desperate and friendless, and even old George, not to mention all the Deep Problems. I saw my parents for the first time through other people's eyes, and I felt strangely proud of them.

Chapter Sixteen

Aftermath

It felt rather eerie doing my paper round next morning. The face of Zac's father glared at me from the front page of every paper I delivered. When I finally got in, I dragged myself upstairs wearily with a cup of coffee for Zac, guessing he would not want eggs and bacon. He looked as sick as a horse that morning, and as he sat up in bed clutching his mug he said, 'Davo, I want to go and see Dad, will you come with me?'

The Fleetbridge Police Station was just about the last place on earth I wanted to go. I even felt sick walking by it with my bag of papers, but old Zac was the only real friend I had ever had, and I couldn't turn him down. So I got Pam to stand in for me in the newsagents and went along with him.

It was a bitter February morning and the steel cold wind stung our faces with sleet. It's not funny having no hair on a day like that. You couldn't very well wear a hat on top of a green mohawkan, and even a woolly pom-pom looked ridiculous.

When we arrived, Zac disappeared into the Holy of Holies with a skinny police constable, and I had to twiddle my thumbs on the hard bench facing the duty sergeant's desk. It was ghastly. The place seemed to crawl with fuzz, answering telephones, pecking at typewriters and dealing with endless enquiries from nutty old ladies.

I saw my 'favourite' sergeant a couple of times too many, and they all seemed to eye me with profound disfavour!

As I sat there I really hated my studs, earrings, tattoos and green hair. 'If I'd have come in here a year ago,' I thought bitterly, 'in my minister's son outfit, with a nice neat haircut and a collar and tie, they'd all be beaming at me now, and probably offering me cups of tea.' But teachers and policemen all see the same. They judge people by what they look like on the outside. Just because I had changed my appearance it did not mean I was different on the *inside*. Or did it? Had it been my inward change that had caused the outward difference?

These philosophical thoughts were getting too deep for me, and I was relieved to see Zac emerging from the bowels of the earth at long last. I knew just what he was going to say, so I said it for him.

'You need a drink,' and taking him firmly by the arm, I marched him towards the nearest pub.

Automatically he flipped his wallet from the pocket of his bodywarmer as I ordered our shorts. Usually it bulged with notes, but today it looked oddly slim.

'It's empty!' he said in a strange voice. 'Empty as hell.' My own wallet was just as skinny after our morning in the pub the previous day; and there was nothing to do but dive for the door, leaving our drinks unpaid for on the counter.

The cold in the street outside kicked us viciously in the teeth. Zac looked blue and pinched and I could not remember when he had last eaten.

Down by the railway station I knew a greasy little cafe where Garry from the Youth Group had a Saturday job. I pushed Zac inside and he huddled into a corner seat still gazing stupidly at his empty wallet. The place smelt of rancid fat and sweat, but Garry grinned at me from behind the glass cases of stale buns.

'Can you stand us two coffees 'til Wednesday?' I asked. 'We're skint.'

'Sorry to hear about Zac's dad,' said Garry as he slurped brown dishwater into our saucers. I felt like saying 'what's a nice boy like you doing in a place like this?' but it was hardly a day for joking.

'This is empty too,' said Zac flapping a cigarette box in my face as I pushed his cup over the dirty table.

'So is mine,' I said soothingly, 'but I'm used to it.'

'You don't understand,' said Zac. 'I've lost everything I ever had, everything's gone – my home, money, Dad, even my future. Do you know what Dad did?'

I had read the papers, but I didn't like to tell him so; it looked nosey. Anyway he did not wait for an answer. 'I knew he ran his own insurance business,' Zac continued bitterly, 'but he's used all the money people invested with him, to import drugs. All those wallies at our house last night – they were his operatives – they were having a planning meeting. Someone must have grassed, and the fuzz swooped on the lot of them. Your sergeant told me all that. He says Dad will never get bail, and I don't suppose he'll get out of prison until he's in his coffin. He owes his clients millions of pounds. Everything we own goes towards paying his debts, the house, cars, the van – everything in the stables right down to the last drum stick. I don't have a thing left in the world. It's all gone.' He looked so broken up, Garry must have been worried about him too because he sidled over with another cup of dishwater and a sagging doughnut.

'Did you see your father?' I said, shovelling as much sugar into his cup as I dared.

'He was poisonous,' spat Zac. 'Anyway, I was so angry with him for mucking up my life, I only stayed with him for a minute.'

124

'But he hasn't mucked up your life,' I said desperately trying to lift his mood. 'You've got a wonderful career lined up in films and television.' He nearly threw his coffee in my face.

'You little tiny twit,' he growled. 'Don't you see, I could only have got into showbiz through his contacts. Now he probably owes them all so much money they won't want to know me.'

'But you can do it in your own right,' I persisted. 'It's you that counts.'

'I'll always be Farroudi's son,' stormed Zac. 'Most of Dad's clients were showbiz people; they'll hate me so much they'll block anything I ever try to do. No! He's ruined my life for me that's what he's done. No one will ever want to know me now.' He picked up his empty wallet and flapped it at me again. 'People only liked me because of this. They were my friends because I could buy them drinks, guitars – anything! Even Mr Atkins would have chucked me out of Gravely years ago if Dad hadn't forked out so well for the school fund and the PTA. When you've got money everyone's your friend, nothing really matters, you've always got the money to keep you safe.'

'That's not why people like you,' I said earnestly.

'Just you watch them now,' he sneered. 'You wait and see.'

He seemed fascinated by his empty wallet, and relapsed into gloomy silence, gazing at it as it lay on the plate by his untouched doughnut.

'You'll have to get a paper round,' I said bracingly, trying to jerk him back to reality.

'Paper round!' he repeated incredulously. 'I couldn't get up at six with my hangovers.'

'Well, if you don't get a job of some kind, you won't be able to afford a hangover,' I said tactlessly. He looked as if I

125

had punched him in the tummy. He seemed to crumple over the table.

'Drink your coffee,' I said hurriedly.

'I had to see some fool social worker in the fuzz house,' he said at last. 'He wanted me to go and live with my Mum.'

'And will you?' I asked curiously.

'No way!' he muttered indignantly.

'Because she's boozy?' I asked.

''Course not. I wouldn't mind that. It's, it's . . . the other thing.'

'She married again then?'

'Married again!' he laughed bitterly. 'No one would take that on. No, I'm not going near her, and if they try and make me, I'll just disappear and that's that.'

'You can stay with us,' I said. 'Mum always wanted ten children, but she only managed to produce me, so she needs lots of people round her to fill the gap.'

'I can't stay with your parents,' Zac sighed. 'I like them too much. I've got no money to pay them.'

'That won't matter,' I laughed. 'They'll just say "the Lord will provide", and He always does.' I found I really believed that as I said it, and I discovered Zac looking at me oddly.

'You just don't add up, Davo,' he said. 'I wonder who you really are inside.' If only I had known, I could have told him.

'Must be dinner time,' I said awkwardly, 'let's go home.'

When we walked into the kitchen at the Manse, Mum was mashing potatoes amid clouds of steam, and Dad was reading the newspaper in his favourite chair. 'It's odd, but they've been married for nearly twenty years, and yet they *still* like just being in the same room.

'Come and have something to eat,' he said looking anxiously at Zac. 'You look as if you need warming up.'

Zac ate his dinner like a clockwork toy, never lifting his eyes from his plate. Dominic and Rosy were there and all the usual jokes and chat went on round him unnoticed. We had almost finished the demolition work on a huge jam suet pudding and John was burping violently with the effort, when Zac suddenly focused his glazed eyes on him, and said vaguely, 'Why d'you keep doing that?' John was too busy chasing a burp up and down his throat to answer, so Dad said, 'John's had a lot of tummy trouble since he came off heroin.'

'You're a junkie?' asked Zac as a flicker of interest crossed his face.

'I'm not now,' said John sounding offended. 'Mr Martin's got me right off it.'

Zac looked round at Dad and stared at him with dull, heavy eyes. 'You any good with drinks trouble?' he said at last.

'You mean alcoholics?' said Dad. 'No, I can't do a thing for them, but I do know someone who can, and I refer them to Him.'

'Is he some kind of a head shrinker?' asked Zac.

'No,' laughed Dad. 'I'm talking about Jesus Christ. He said He'd come to set the prisoners free, and any addiction is a kind of prison, isn't it?'

'How can someone who's dead help people now?' asked Zac.

'But He's not dead,' said Manda from the far side of the table. 'People killed Him, but He was God and so He rose again. He lives in this house, can't you feel Him?' Zac looked nervously over his shoulder and turned his shirt collar up round his ears. John took a dose of his white stomach medicine and said, 'He takes away the desire for the stuff, and makes you strong enough to resist it. Honest He does.' But Zac had had enough for one day, and

127

retreated hastily to our bedroom and promptly fell asleep. There was nothing else for me to do but lie on my own bed and read a book for the first time in months. I have to admit I thoroughly enjoyed it.

It was just after six when the Anarchists came. I heard the irate pounding on the front door when I came downstairs to make myself a mug of tea.

''ere, what's happening?' demanded Steve, before I'd finished opening the door. 'Where's Zac?'

'He's asleep,' I squeaked nervously.

'I'll give 'im sleep!' said Steve menacingly, and he pushed me out of the way and they all surged into the hall after him. Michelle looked round at the shabby furniture and sniffed, while Devil sent our cat leaping for cover. I could not take them into the kitchen because Mum had suddenly decided to spring clean the larder. Dad was in the study preparing Sunday's sermons, and Pam and John had the telly blaring in the sitting room. So there was nothing else I could do but hustle them all up to my attic.

I had left Zac looking like Sleeping Beauty, but by the time we arrived he was awake, sitting cross-legged on my desk, wary as a cat. It was ridiculous getting ten people into that tiny room, even the walls were groaning in protest.

'We want to know what's going on,' demanded Steve truculently, as he thrust his angry face at Zac. 'We've just been round to the stable, and the fuzz turned us away, said we couldn't touch anything in the place.'

'So?' answered Zac without emotion.

'We've got a charity dinner down in Brighton tonight, or has it slipped your memory?' blustered Steve.

'What'll they think if we don't turn up?' put in Tess.

'They'll just have to cry their poor little eyes out, won't they?' replied Zac coldly.

'But they won't ask us again if we let them down,'

persisted Tess. But Zac only shrugged and I could see his attitude was rubbing them all up the wrong way.

'They won't even let me have my van,' bleated Big Jim from the pillow end of my bed where he'd subsided. He is just like a huge bouncy puppy, but that day he seemed to have lost his bone.

'It never was *your* van,' snarled Zac, 'and what d'you suppose it's like for me. I can't even get into the house for clean underpants.'

'But all our lovely gear,' said Simon who looked close to tears.

'You're just going to have to start paying for your own gear now,' hissed Zac. There was a stunned silence while this information sank in.

'But it would cost thousands,' said Simon at last blinking miserably behind his glasses.

Suddenly a minor explosion occurred in the corner of the room. 'I've had an idea!' shouted Big Jim as he shot off my bed rather like an RAF pilot in his ejector seat.

'Shut up you lot,' said Steve sarcastically. 'He's never had an idea in his life before.'

Big Jim ignored him, and continued excitedly, 'Do you know my girlfriend?'

'Never knew you had one,' said Tess nastily. 'She blind as well as nutty?' Nothing ever ruffles Big Jim and he went on ignoring the giggles and titters.

'She works in the music shop in Mill Street, and she told me that if we ever wanted anything it wouldn't be hard to get it.'

'You mean she'd smuggle a drum stick home in her tights,' grinned Trev.

'They've got a staff lav out the back,' continued Jim, above the sniggers. 'She just might forget to shut the window one evening, and someone could climb in and open the back door.' Trev went straight into a brilliant demonstration of a robot crawling through a small window, and getting his head stuck in the loo, but Simon's eyes were suddenly gleaming behind his glasses. 'They've got everything we could ever need in that shop,' he said, licking his lips. 'I spend hours in there just looking.'

'All those shops in Mill Street back on to Farthing Lane, no one would see a van up there on a dark night.' The mocking smile had faded from Steve's face, and it was sharp with interest.

'We haven't got a van any more,' pointed out Monkey.

'We could nick one for a night,' beamed Jim. No one had ever listened to him before – this was his finest hour.

'But if we got all the gear, where would we keep it?' continued the ever cautious Monkey.

'No hassle!' said Simon, cleaning his glasses on his oil-stained hankie. 'My workshop! It's only an old garage at the bottom of our garden, but no one ever goes in there, and even if Mum did, I'd tell her it was school stuff I'm doing up.'

'Have you all gone out of your tiny minds?' Zac's voice cut across the buzz of excitement like an ice-cold bucket of water. 'The fuzz aren't fools, they'll soon have a description of all the gear and the serial numbers. They'll be sniffing at every gig in the district.'

'No hassle,' repeated Simon. 'I put the amplifiers into new cases and respray the instruments.'

'Well you can count me out of the whole thing,' growled Zac.

'Chicken are you?' demanded Steve.

'I had to go and see my Dad down at the pigs' sty, do you really think I'm keen to join him?'

'So you'll leave us to take all the risks, and then come in for all the glory – as usual!' sneered Steve.

'No,' answered Zac evenly. 'I meant count me out for ever. I'm sick of the lot of you.' There was a stunned silence. We all knew that meant curtains for the Anarchists. Without Zac's genius, we would only be schoolkids messing about.

'You can't just switch people off when it suits you,' raged Steve.

'Well I just did it,' answered Zac, 'so why don't you all shove off, you're using up too much oxygen.'

'I'll give you oxygen!' stormed Steve. 'You think if you're not paying for everything you won't be number one.'

Zac probably hates violence as much as I do, and I've never seen him exert himself physically before, but something inside him seemed to snap then, and uncurling his legs he lunged at Steve from the height of my desk and punched him hard on the side of his rugged face. Steve who was taken completely by surprise fell backwards on top of Simon, who squeaked like an indignant mouse.

'I'll kill you for that!' threatened Steve, but before he could move, Devil decided to do the job for him. With a snarl that I have heard in my nightmares often since, he sprang at Zac ripping open the front of his shirt. I could see by Steve's face that he had no intention of calling Devil off, and I panicked. I never had trusted that dog. Wildly I looked round the room for something to use as a weapon, and there, on the windowsill stood my hair spray. I grabbed it and fired the aerosol into the animal's savage face. Sneezing and choking he retired under my desk, but Steve was on his feet again and had Zac by the throat. The girls screamed and Simon hid his face in my pillow. We all knew what it meant when Steve lost his cool.

In many ways Big Jim resembles Devil, and instantly he sprang at Steve, in much the same way as the dog had defended *his* master.

Once again Steve was taken off guard, and the two huge bodies careered across the room crashing against the wall. My old Gran's picture of the 'Light of the World' descended on their heads like a guillotine, covering the tangle of arms and legs with a shower of broken glass.

At that unfortunate moment, the door was forced open and there stood Dad, still clutching his sermon notes in his hand.

'You are all very welcome in my house,' he said quietly, 'but I would be most grateful if you could make less noise.'

'I'm sorry,' muttered Zac, 'they're all going now, and they *won't* be coming back.'

'Good job you came up when you did,' I said as Dad and I stood at the top of the stairs watching the Anarchists slinking down into the hall below. Then we both looked back into my bedroom and saw a strange sight. Zac, who was always so mature and sophisticated had collapsed on his bed and was crying like a baby. I fled downstairs, prickling all over with embarrassment, leaving him to Dad who, after all, is very good at coping with things like that.

Chapter Seventeen

A New Zac

The worst part of a paper round is missing a Sunday lie in, but I usually crawled back into bed after my hot rolls and honey. Zac snored away all that morning as if he had to catch up on months of sleep, and I wondered what on earth he and Dad had talked about up here the night before. I'd even had to suffer *Match of the Day*.

Just as I reached the satisfactory climax of the book I had started the day before, I was roused to reality by the smell of roast beef wafting up from the kitchen, and I gave Zac a prod.

'Lunch time,' I shouted in his ear.

'Get off,' he protested, 'I'm not hungry.'

The wails and squeals of Kevin greeted me as I walked downstairs, and I could not help feeling glad Zac was still in bed. It would be better for him to settle down in the Manse for a few days before we sprang Kevin on him. Zac was so fastidious about everything that surrounded him, I felt instinctively that Kevin would revolt him.

I actually managed to get a seat by Manda, just being close to her made the world feel safe again, but she was preoccupied that day by Joan, Kevin's mother, who looked as if she had been crying. My heart sank. I simply could not face any more deep problems.

Dad had just finished carving the joint, and Mum was fussing round with the vegetables when a most unusual hush fell on everybody. I followed everyone else's gaze to the doorway, and there stood Zac, staring at Kevin with a look of shocked horror all over his face. I felt irritated. I know Kevin takes some swallowing, but there was no need to overreact quite so violently. Secretly, I was very proud of the way Manda treated him. But as I looked from Zac to Kevin, something went click in my brain, and catching Dad's eye, I knew that he had also remembered who Zac was like.

'What are you two doing here?' demanded Zac turning furiously on the astonished Joan.

'They're friends of ours,' said Dad gently.

'Why didn't you tell me that?' asked Zac.

'We didn't know you knew each other.'

'Know her!' shouted Zac. 'She's my mother, and *that*,' he added pointed to the shrivelled and distorted image of himself, 'is my twin brother. Typical of them to come here and spoil everything.' He slammed out of the room while Joan burst into tears and Kevin wailed in sympathy.

We sat round the dinner table in a state of shock. Snatches of conversation I'd had with Zac came floating back to me as I struggled to fit the missing pieces of my mental jigsaw together again. Joan cried quietly into her hankie, while Kevin rocked to and fro in his wheelchair whimpering unhappily, sensing that his mother was upset.

The only person who was quite unconcerned was George. He is so deaf he had not really understood what was going on, but he seized his opportunity and quickly helped himself to far more than his share of roast potatoes and Yorkshire puddings, and hastily began to eat with greedy enjoyment while his chin waved up and down violently.

'You know about my husband, I suppose,' sobbed Joan at last.

'Well, it's all been in the papers hasn't it?' said Dad, 'but of course we had no idea you had any connection with Mr Farroudi.'

'I've used my maiden name since I left him,' explained Joan, 'and that was six years ago.'

'Have you seen much of Zac since then?' asked Dad.

'He won't come near us,' she replied bitterly. 'He's the same as his father – they just can't accept Kevin,' and she burst into a fresh wave of tears. Mum hastily passed some paper napkins down the table like pass the parcel at a kiddies' party.

'Zachary has grown up into such a lovely looking boy hasn't he,' sighed Joan, while her eyes rested on Kevin. Somehow his handicap seemed more of a tragedy when you saw what he might have been.

'Where's he going to live now?' she asked, looking suddenly worried. 'I couldn't possibly cope with him.'

'Zac can stay here with us,' said Mum comfortably, 'and we'll all pray that he learns to accept Kevin soon.'

'It's my fault he feels the way he does,' said Joan. She was a quiet, rather withdrawn person usually, but today her dam had burst and she didn't seem able to stop talking. 'When the twins were born, Kevin was so delicate he took up all my time. Zachary just had to get on with it. I used to prop his bottle up on a cushion and let him feed himself. It took hours just getting a few ounces of milk into Kevin. When Zachary grew into such an energetic, naughty little boy I just couldn't manage him, and their father was so busy building his empire he was never at home. That's why I started drinking.' We were all so used to people's problems served like gravy with every meal, that we were not as embarrassed as we might have been, but no one felt they could just start eating, even though this was the only decent meal we had in the week. So we all sat and let it get cold on the plates in front of us, while George helped himself to a third helping.

'Joan,' said Dad in response to a look from Mum, 'let's go into the study and talk about this.'

'No,' she said blowing her nose with finality. 'Sundays are busy days for you, you need your dinner, and I must give Kevin something. I can't have him getting upset.'

I felt cross that she did not care at all about Zac going hungry, so I offered to take his meal upstairs. Mum shot me a grateful smile, but actually I was glad to escape. John was belching with shock and George was getting up my nose in more ways than one.

When I kicked open the bedroom door, Zac was sitting on the floor in the corner, his knees hugged under his chin. He always sits like that when he's upset.

'Take that away, I'm not hungry,' he snapped.

'I can't take it down again,' I said. 'Mum gets terribly stirred up if people don't eat what she cooks. She feels they're rejecting *her*.' I knew that would work. Zac was desperately anxious to get on well with my parents.

'How long's *she* been hanging round here?' Zac asked, as he plunged his fork unenthusiastically into a potato.

'They've been coming here several times a week for a couple of years now. Doctor Davidson asked Mum to visit them one day because he thought he should get Kevin into a home. Joan had got so she didn't dare go out and she was drinking herself paralytic, so Mum prayed hard and God did a miracle.'

'Pity He bothered,' growled Zac.

'But she's changed so much, you've no idea what she used to be like.'

'Yes I have,' snapped Zac. 'I know *just* what she used to be like. She hated me, and only cared about Kevin and her gin.'

The door opened very slowly and Manda lurched into the room. Somehow, by a superhuman effort, she had managed to get upstairs with two bowls of apple tart on a tray, and her face was scarlet with the effort. I watched the thunder-clouds dispersing rapidly from Zac's face, and I sensed that Manda was just about the only girl he liked, and the realisation certainly did not fill me with pleasure.

'How would *you* feel if you had a twin brother who needed his nappies changing?' he asked her abruptly. I felt he needed her approval and was trying to justify his feelings. Manda is a transparently honest person; she always says exactly what she is thinking.

'I'd feel sad for him,' she replied candidly, collapsing on the end of my bed, exhausted from her mountaineering feat.

'Every time I look at him,' said Zac moodily, 'I feel bad. I can move, talk, go where I like, while he sits there dribbling all day. He makes me feel guilty just for being alive.'

'But it wasn't *your* fault he was born brain-damaged,' said Manda. 'He *may* just sit and dribble, but he knows when someone loves him, and responds in his own way. He won't eat his dinner today, because he knows his Mum's upset. When you get to know him you won't be able to help loving him. Just because he and I are disabled, it doesn't mean we're not people you know.' Zac and I both gazed at her, startled by the intensity of her feelings.

'It wasn't fair,' said Zac thoughtfully, 'you getting hit by that car and not Mary; and Kevin and I were both born at the same time. Why should he end up like he is? You're always on about God round here, but why does He let things like that happen?'

'How should I know?' laughed Manda. 'I'd be God Himself if I did. But I do know that Kevin won't always be stuck in that chair. When he gets to Heaven he'll be able to walk and talk and enjoy life. I never realised until I had the accident just how short life is—it's only a fragment of our real existence. Eternity goes on for ever. We think our lives

137

are so important, we almost demand that they're happy and easy. But God's looking at us from the other side of time, and He knows what wonderful things He is planning for us one day.'

'That's all very well,' growled Zac, 'but what if a person's not good enough to get into Heaven, what then?'

'No one's good enough to go there,' said Manda unexpectedly. 'Do you realise just what Mary and I were doing at Gravely last year? We were blackmailing people. Do you remember that vicar's daughter, Jessica James? We smashed her life up so badly, she's still in a mental hospital, and she wasn't the only person we destroyed either. There's no way God could let me into Heaven, but I know for sure I am going there.'

'How can you know that?' asked Zac uneasily, and I sensed he was still worrying about Joe.

'No one can go to Heaven who has ever done anything wrong,' she replied, 'so that shuts us all out! But God punished Jesus instead of us, so if we tell Him we're sorry for the things we do, and accept the fact that He died in our place, then we can be *sure* of getting to Heaven.'

'This is all getting too much for me,' said Zac wearily. 'I'm going back to sleep,' and he curled himself up on his bed and pulled the duvet over his head.

I read another whole book that day, and Zac never stirred once until about nine when Dad walked in carrying a tray of cocoa and biscuits. He always has that when he comes in from church. Sitting down on my bed he looked anxiously at Zac over the rim of his steaming mug.

'Wake up,' I said, 'thumping him on the back, 'you're not a hibernating hedgehog.'

'I've come to ask for your help Zac,' said Dad when he had handed him his cocoa.

'*My* help?' said Zac incredulously.

138

'It's Easter Sunday five weeks today, and I want to do something completely different this year – shake everyone up a bit. I've asked the Youth Group to do a Passion Play during the morning service.'

'A Passion Play?' repeated Zac, trying to shake the sleep out of his head.

'Hundreds of years ago when most people couldn't read the Bible, strolling players used to go round the markets and towns acting plays based on the Bible.'

'Oh yes,' said Zac suddenly enthusiastic, 'that was *real* theatre, just an old cart and a few props – they must really have known how to act in those days.' Dad smiled at him, and I sensed that he liked Zac as much as I did.

'I've asked them to do a play about the crucifixion and resurrection of Jesus. They were wildly enthusiastic about the idea when I talked to them after church just now, but they'll only do it on one condition.' Zac was munching a digestive biscuit and had lost interest in the conversation.

'They want *you* to produce it.'

'Me!' said Zac spluttering biscuit crumbs all over his bed.

'Yes, your reputation as a producer seems to be high in Fleetbridge,' laughed Dad.

'But I can't just move in and organise people I don't know,' protested Zac.

'But you *do* know most of them from school, and they've asked for you specifically. In fact, they won't attempt it without you.'

'But I don't know anything about Jesus Christ,' objected Zac.

'You could read it up,' encouraged Dad. 'It would mean a lot to me if you did it. There's just no one else who could.'

What was Dad's game I wondered. Did he really want a Passion Play, or was he just giving Zac something new to live for? He had been so down recently he certainly did need something like this to remotivate him. And I could just imagine Dad getting the whole Youth Group praying for Zac.

'They're all at Mike's house now. Why don't you come down with me and meet them – kick a few ideas around?'

'You coming, Davo?' asked Zac cautiously.

'No way,' I said definitely. 'I'm not getting mixed up with that lot again.' Zac hesitated, torn between me and his deep desire to placate my father.

'Manda will be there,' said Dad quietly. It was only a subtle little carrot but it worked. Dad is nobody's fool.

It was the middle of the night when I woke up, feeling cross because the light was still on. I saw such an extraordinary sight I nearly fell out of bed with surprise. There was Zac, sitting up reading my Bible!

'This thing's going to work!' he said excitedly. 'What a story! It's got such dramatic potential I can't wait to get at it.' From that night he changed completely. His depression was gone – he was alert, and full of energy and enthusiasm. If this is what Dad had planned, his idea had certainly worked.

Chapter Eighteen

An Uncertain Future

'It's not too late David.' I jumped violently. I had thought I was alone in the room. Miss Carmichael had left with everyone else at the end of the geography lesson, but she must have come back for something and found me staring blankly out of the window.

'I said it's not too late,' she repeated. 'The exams are still more than three months away; if you started working again and really got your nose down, you could do well.' I looked at her sharply. Was she being rude about my nose?

'Look, this is your last chance David, but you could still do it.' I must have looked a wally standing there staring at her, but I was in the middle of yet another identity crisis, and Gravely had seemed a very lonely place that week. The Anarchists were constantly huddled in their corner of the common room discussing their plans in whispers. I felt it was rather disloyal to Zac if I joined them, so I kept out of the room altogether. Zac had been entirely submerged by the CU and they never stopped talking about their wretched Passion Play. They were all very friendly to me, but I could spot their little game a mile off – they wanted to pull me back into their group again. But for me that would have meant climbing down and admitting I'd been wrong ever to turn my back on them. Now here was Miss Carmichael offering me a way out of the vacuum in which my life was suspended.

'I'll help you all I can,' she said, 'and I'll encourage other members of staff to do the same.'

'Thank you,' I said, feeling rather dazed. 'Thank you very much.'

The rest of that term rocketed by, as I retreated like a snail into my attic shell catching up on my school work almost round the clock. I even gave up my paper rounds and Saturday job, but I still got up at six so I could revise for two hours before breakfast. I can't say I enjoyed it. I felt miserably isolated, and often my brain positively ached, but there was a strange satisfaction in rebuilding my life, making something decent out of it at last. I didn't need God, my parents, or Zac and the Anarchists for that matter.

But all the noise and laughter that I could hear going on in the house below me, added to my loneliness and I scarcely saw Zac. His passionate love for drama was as catching as 'flu and soon he was working with a cast of over fifty, not to mention all the people who were making costumes and props, planning the temporary stage, and all the lighting effects. Suddenly something that Dad had imagined as a five-minute slot before the sermon had become a major church objective, and he was as excited as everyone else.

When Zac was not rehearsing in the hall, he was sitting up half the night writing scripts, stage directions or simply reading my Bible. 'This is so good for my technique,' he said. 'With a cast this big, everything has to be written down. It's a new kind of drama for me.' I think he must have given up sleep for Lent!

I hated the meal times most of all, they were nothing but noisy committee meetings, and I felt miserably left out. Manda was always trying to bring me into the conversation, but even she was becoming maddeningly involved.

'Zac,' she said one evening over burnt mince and soggy

rice, 'Even if you don't seem to care about exams yourself, you might at least give the rest of us a bit of time off to revise.' She had not wanted to be in the play at first, saying, 'You can't have an actress who hobbles round the stage with a walking stick.'

'Yes you can,' Zac had replied. 'I'm casting you as Mary, and she'd have been quite old by then, so you can hobble all you like.' John was going to be Pontius Pilate, because Zac said it was probably a show of good manners for a Roman to burp.

'Are you playing a part in this play, Zachary?' asked Joan. Poor woman, she was trying so hard to be friendly, but she *would* talk to Zac as if he'd been a little boy, and the aggro between them was increasing and not diminishing at all.

'No way,' drawled Zac without looking at her. 'I'm not a Christian.'

'Actually he acts everyone's part to show us how to do them,' laughed Manda.

'Who's playing Jesus?' I asked curiously.

There was an awkward pause, and then Zac replied at last, 'Dominic's doing it.'

'What, with all that acne?' I laughed derisively.

'Oh, we'll plaster him with make-up and give him a false beard, he'll *look* all right, but . . . well, he's a bit wooden.'

'If you had a mother like his, you'd be wooden yourself,' giggled Pam. But I could see Zac was worried.

'Pity Dan's not here,' I said watching carefully for Manda's reaction. 'He'd do it perfectly.' But Manda was too busy gazing at Zac to notice what I had said. Was it just my imagination or was she spending rather too much of her time looking at Zac? I couldn't really blame her. He did look magnificent and he still had all his fabulous clothes. She'd never fancy me now, I knew I looked a mess. Without any money to maintain my hair the green dye had grown out, so I'd lopped off my fringe with Mum's scissors and my own mousy brown hair was sticking through the tattoos. I was so run down physically, my spots were worse than ever, and the ring in my nose had turned septic.

'Come on you lot,' urged Zac, 'stop gassing, we're due at the hall for a rehearsal.'

'Slave driver,' complained Pam.

'Well you can't say he doesn't work hard himself,' said Dad.

'My feet never touch the ground these days,' laughed Zac happily, 'and I haven't had time to go near a pub for weeks!' He hurtled out of the room, but I distinctly saw Dad and Manda wink at each other.

'You've just got to be mad, Davo,' said Zac erupting into my room about midnight that evening. He flung his clipboard down on the bed, and sprang on to my desk, scattering my history papers and knocking over the ink.

'Mad?' I said wearily, putting down my pen.

'How could you ever walk out on all that lot over at church, get yourself all messed up by us Anarchists with all our problems?'

'Problems?' I said blankly.

'Yes, we're all nothing but bad news.'

'Well, we've got plenty of problems here,' I argued. 'What about Manda, and have you met Dominic's mother?'

'Yes,' said Zac thoughtfully, 'but they're so happy, things don't pull them down. I've never met people like this before, I can't understand what operates them. Usually in drama groups everyone wants the best parts, and you have everyone bitching at everyone else and masses of aggro. If anything goes wrong, this lot just pray about it. It's uncanny Davo, but it always works. They all seem to like each other – they even like *me*, *without* my money! In the Anarchists, we just hated one another really.'

'Don't be a wally,' I said crossly, but I knew just what he meant. I had felt the difference when I first joined the Anarchists, but the other way on. I knew the Youth Group were different because they had God living in their lives. Had He ever actually lived in mine, or had I just known about Him on the outside? My old Gran had been dead for several months by then, but her wretched little sayings kept coming back to haunt me like ghosts in white sheets. 'If we haven't that *within* us, that is *above* us, we will soon yield to that which is *around* us.' 'Silly old bat!' I thought crossly. I'd show them all I could be my own person.

Zac dived off my desk, on to his bed and was asleep before I could peel off my jeans. It wasn't much fun being lonely.

The moment that I had been dreading arrived the following day.

'We need your help,' whispered Steve. He had tracked me to the school library at the end of the afternoon, and now his huge body was towering over my chair. He'd had his bush of hair dyed raven black and his eyebrows plucked – he looked terrible.

'We're doing it on Thursday night,' he continued when he had made sure no one was listening. 'That way the job won't be discovered until the shop opens again after Easter, which'll give Si a chance to pick the stuff over before the fuzz get busy.' I felt sick and cold all over.

'I don't think I'd better help,' I said, as the image of my police sergeant floated into my head. 'The pigs are watching me closely since I nicked the collection money.'

'We don't want you in Mill Street,' he grinned. 'You'd get in the way. We need you to work on Zac. We're gambling *everything* on him coming back when we get some gear. We'll never make a go of it without him, and we need you too.'

His words echoed and re-echoed in my burning ears. 'We need you.' No one else did. My fingers itched for the feel of a guitar again, and my soul bulged with unwritten songs.

'I'll work on Zac,' I promised. 'Once this wretched play is over on Sunday, he'll be bored to tears again.' Steve had never looked at me so pleasantly before.

'All we need is a really good keyboard player,' he said, 'then we can do another demo tape. We'll have a contract with a record company in no time.'

Could there really be a future out there after all? I shovelled my books into my school bag. 'Good luck for Thursday!' I hissed. 'Leave Zac to me.'

But talking to Zac was much easier said than done. During that last week before Easter, the house positively pulsated with people, the 'phone and the doorbell never stopped ringing and Zac was the eye of the storm. The church was invaded by amateur carpenters and electricians, and Dad's hopes of 'shaking everyone up a bit' were certainly being realised. When the television company rang to ask if they could film some of this 'modern Passion Play' for ITV news, he sounded delighted. He had already given permission for it all to be videoed and several newspaper reporters and photographers wanted to attend the production. 'Half of Fleetbridge say they are coming,' he laughed. 'We'll have to take the roof off the church to hold them all.'

It was Easter Saturday evening, and I had spent most of it looking gloomily out of my attic bedroom window. The church blazed with light for the final dress rehearsal, and all day long it had been full of noise and activity as the last minute arrangements had been made. Then I watched the entire cast, technicians, stage hands and the make-up and wardrobe people all surging over to the Manse. Mum's eyes would be gleaming with pleasure as she served them refreshments from a kitchen table that positively sagged under the weight of her soggy baking.

Suddenly my attic seemed unbearably empty and I went downstairs just in time to see a hilarious sight. Everyone was squashing themselves into the sitting room for a prayer meeting about the Passion Play, and poor old Zac was drawn in with them, obviously quite unaware of what they were going to do. I positively cracked up, and sat myself down on the stairs so I could watch the door for the first sight of the expression on his face when he managed to escape.

My long wait was rewarded. His face was the colour of school chalk and he was one of the first to erupt from the room.

'Cor Davo!' he said springing up the stairs and slumping down beside me, 'I've never been to anything like that before.' The Youth Group surged round the front hall at our feet while Mum poked the leftover food at them, and I cackled with laughter.

'How much will you give me *not* to tell Steve and Tess you spent an hour and a half in a prayer meeting?'

'I haven't any money to bribe you with,' he laughed, 'but I'll kill you if you do, and I mean it. Funny thing,' he added thoughtfully, 'but they talk to God as if He was producing this play and not me, and when your Dad or Manda start praying it feels like God's right in the room – so you could almost touch Him.'

I suddenly realised that first time in weeks I had his full attention. Was this my chance to deliver Steve's message?

'Zac,' I said, 'have you thought what you're going to do after all this is over?' He looked up at me, startled, and then a bleak expression shadowed his eyes, so I pressed my advantage. 'Suppose we'd got hold of some really good gear . . .'

147

'We?'

'The Anarchists,' I answered impatiently.

Zac looked down on to all the happy people swirling round below us, and he said, 'Davo, I wouldn't go back and work with the Anarchists if they had a contract for their own TV programme.'

'But listen ...' I began urgently, but someone in the crowd shouted, 'Zac, there's someone here from ITV and they want to see you about camera positions.'

Zac was up and off in an instant and I was left with positively nothing. A wave of despair washed over me, and I rested my forehead on my knees in hopeless defeat. Sometimes loneliness can hurt like a physical pain.

Someone put a hand on my shoulder. I knew just who it was without looking up, and my whole body began to burn.

'David,' said Manda gently, 'why are you doing this to yourself?' I looked up into her face, and realised with a stab of longing that she was beautiful. Suddenly other faces looked back at me through the years – all of them were Manda's – each one was like a stepping stone of my love for her.

The first day I had arrived at Gravely, convinced everyone would laugh at me because I was so small, Manda had met me in the corridor and smiled, making me feel I was a real person and not a freak.

Then I saw another face, white, twisted with fear, looking at me appealingly from the back of a police car swirling out of the school gates. 'She's been pushing drugs round the school,' said a smug voice from the crowd. Everything in me had wanted to shout 'No! She's just become a Christian, she couldn't do a thing like that. She's been framed!' I had longed to protect her – fight for her, but the police car forced her away from me.

When had I first realised I loved her? Was it the day she

had stood in the common room doorway on her first morning back at school trying so hard not to cry? I was not sure. All I did know was that I loved her now, and I would love her for the rest of my life. In spite of all the cruel things life had thrown at her, or maybe because of them, her face was lit by an inner strength and peace that made her stand out, head and shoulders above anyone else I had ever known.

'David, you're so miserable,' she said, and her arm was still round me. 'You don't have to be.' She was looking at me with love in her eyes, but I knew she wanted to draw me towards God and not herself. I longed to tell her just how I felt about her, but I had done that once before, and I felt I would fall apart if I was rejected again. It was Zac she really loved now, it could never be me.

'I wish you were in the Passion Play,' she continued. 'It would have been so lovely if you could have written a song to round it all off at the end. I always used to love it when you sang.'

'I'm too far away from God now,' I croaked despairingly.

'Once I heard my Aunt Beth say, "even if we travel a thousand steps away from God, we only have to turn and take one step back towards Him because He's been walking behind us all the way."'

'Manda, I must talk to you . . .' But my usual bad luck held, and Pam came out of the kitchen with a mug of coffee in her hand and plonked her fat giggling body down on the step below us. The doorbell went and the telephone rang and once again, I was in a world full of busy people who had no time to stop and listen to me.

Chapter Nineteen

The Passion Play

I came downstairs the following morning to find that pandemonium had broken out. The entire household was standing in the kitchen all talking at once and ignoring the hot rolls and chocolate Easter eggs that lay invitingly on the breakfast table. John was actually wringing his hands and Pam was crying loudly.

'What's up?' I asked helping myself to a roll, and feeling rather like George.

'Dominic's mother's just rung up to say he's got a cold and she's keeping him in bed,' explained Manda.

'Typical of her!' exploded Pam in disgust, 'it's probably only a little snuffle.'

'Well he must be nearly seventeen,' I said scornfully, 'why doesn't he just tell the old battleaxe to get knotted?'

'He tried that,' hiccoughed Pam, 'so she's locked him in his bedroom. She's impossible.'

'Poor old Dominic,' said Dad gently. 'He'll feel so bad letting us all down.'

'Yes but what are we going to *do*?' roared John with a belch that would have been worthy of Caesar himself.

'There's only one person who could take his part, and that's you Zac,' said Manda quietly. 'After all you've acted it enough times trying to show him how to do it.'

'Oh no!' said Zac looking genuinely frightened. 'I'm not acting in this play.'

'But you must!' pleaded Pam. 'The TV cameramen will be here any minute.'

'Look,' said Zac, 'I can only act when I'm three parts drunk.'

'You'll just have to rely on the Holy Spirit and not your vodka this time,' laughed Dad.

'Best thing that could have happened,' I said cramming my mouth full of chocolate egg. 'Dominic was bound to be lousy in the part anyway. You do it Zac and you'll *make* the whole thing.'

But Zac was backing away from us, into the corner of the kitchen. He looked like a terrified animal cornered in a trap.

'You don't understand,' he said looking appealingly round at us, 'I can't play Jesus, I'm not . . . I'm not the right kind of person. I've done things . . . bad things . . . I couldn't . . .' Dad put his hand gently on Zac's shoulder as he said, 'Zac, the greatest saint the world has ever produced would never be worthy to play that part. Would you let me ask Jesus right now to give you the courage to do this to please Him?' Zac stood staring at him as the wild look died slowly from his dark eyes, then without a word he bowed his head. I never thought I'd see Zac Farroudi actually praying.

The silence in the house felt suffocating. Everyone had gone over to the church and I was alone. They had all been far too preoccupied to ask me if I was going over to watch the production. Of course, I would have said no if they *had* asked me, but all the same I felt left out and forgotten.

I climbed slowly upstairs to my attic, and tried to settle down to my maths revision, but my eyes kept wandering to the window where I could see people converging on the church from every direction and parked cars were practically blocking all the roads in the vicinity. Outside the church stood a huge ITV van and all the neighbours were standing at their windows or in their gardens not wanting to miss the excitement. So why was I shut up here with only my maths for company? Suddenly I threw down my pen in disgust and dived downstairs at full speed. Anyone might be curious, I told myself, as I walked up to the church door. I wasn't capitulating to God, I was just being nosey. Anyway, the Church Deacons probably wouldn't let me in, in case I nicked the collection bag again. But the two men who handed out the hymn books at the door gave me such a warm welcome, I felt just like a VIP.

'There's not a seat left in the place,' they beamed, 'but you'll get a lovely view if you stand here at the back with us.'

I shall never forget walking into church that morning. The atmosphere positively hit me in the face. The play had obviously been going on for some time, because the audience was already deeply involved. It almost felt as if the church was empty, the silence was so profound. Not a cough or a fidget, they were riveted. The windows had been blacked out, and the whole place was in darkness except where the fierce spotlights were trained on to the temporary stage.

A dark blue curtain formed a backdrop and with a few cardboard pillars and the odd bit of draped fabric the set looked so authentically Roman, you could almost see the mosaic floor.

'What is truth?' sneered John, standing in the centre of the stage in his full Roman regalia and cleverly disguising a burp by pretending to clear his throat.

Zac stood before him, his hands bound behind his back. A small insignificant peasant, surrounded by the rich grandeur of Rome. Yet because of his uncanny ability to act, he held the undivided attention of everyone in that building. He never acts a part, he simply *becomes* the person he is portraying.

His casting had also been brilliant. He had put people's natural personalities as well as their physical failings to the best possible use. The costumes were magic, but the sound effects were rather too realistic for comfort. When they dragged Zac off the stage after Pilate's order to scourge him, a gasp of horror ran through the audience as the sound of the ghastly whips filled our ears. One of the Deacons who was standing beside me was a local butcher, and the other a bus driver, but they both allowed the tears to run down their cheeks unchecked.

'I never knew it had to be like that,' muttered the butcher blowing his nose.

Pilate paced up and down on the stage, nervously biting his finger nails and mopping the sweat from his face, while the terrible noise continued off stage. Suddenly his wife (Pam) rushed hysterically across the stage.

'Let this good man go,' she screamed. 'I have suffered all night with dreams about him.' But just at that minute, the soldiers dragged Zac back on stage again, and there was a ripple of horror from the already uncomfortable audience. I don't know who was in charge of their make-up, but Michelle herself could not have done better. Zac was stripped to the waist revealing a back that was crossed and recrossed with ghastly wounds, and when he struggled to his feet and turned to look at us, his face was also streaked with blood from the crown of thorns. It was impossible *not* to believe he was actually Jesus, standing there forsaken and alone.

'Crucify him!' yelled the crowd, and Zac's expressive face winced with the pain of their rejection. I had to bite my lip until it bled to stop myself joining the two weeping Deacons.

But how on earth is he going to manage the actual crucifixion, I thought. Surely that will be an anticlimax. But I might have known Zac would have worked out a solution even for that problem.

Someone had made a huge cross from roughly sawn wood, and Garry (who was Simon of Cyrene) lugged it on to the stage after Zac had collapsed under its weight while struggling down the church aisle. The soldiers roughly threw him down on to it, and when they were standing round we could not properly see what was happening. But we heard the gruesome sound of those hammers all right, and when Zac gasped, 'Father forgive them, they don't know what they are doing,' it really hurt the audience physically.

I think they must actually have tied him to the cross with ropes and there was a small ledge just large enough for his feet. But all the same it had to be a terrifying experience for Zac as they hauled the cross up by ropes from the rafters and left him suspended nine feet above the stage.

The church was completely dark with just one spot on Zac's agonised face. I think his performance that day deserved a hundred Oscars.

Because of the sheer horror of that dark scene the resurrection came as an enormous relief, and people could not stop themselves from jumping up all over the church and clapping one another on the back and shaking hands. When the whole thing was over Dad came on stage and said, 'It is not necessary or even possible for me to preach a sermon after that. I believe we have seen today just how much it cost the Lord Jesus to die in our places and take our punishment. All we can do now is to respond to His great love for us.'

I pushed hastily through the swing doors behind me and fled. During that performance everything within me wanted to respond to God, especially at the very end when Zac had stood in the centre of the stage holding out his arms and saying, 'Come unto me all you who labour and are heavily burdened, and I will give you rest.' Manda had said you only have to take one step back towards God, and I nearly took it, but then I remembered it would mean climbing down publicly, telling Dad and Mum I'd been wrong and crawling back to church like a whimpering dog. I couldn't do that. So I pushed my way out of church before I was brainwashed any further.

Outside in the cold air I paused. I was shaking all over and my throat felt as if I had swallowed a hedgehog. 'I must go round to the hall' I thought, 'and congratulate Zac on his production. He's put so much effort into it.'

As I slipped in through the side door I was conscious of something very strange. After any performance there is always a great release of tension; people laugh and crack jokes and discuss the technical side of their acting, but an almost reverent hush filled the hall. They were simply changing silently and slipping back into church, so absorbed by what they had been doing that they seemed almost dazed. I stood with my back against the wall as one by one they crept past me, until soon only Manda was left, still dressed in her blue Mary costume, staring fixedly into space.

'That really was something,' I said sitting down beside her.

'Zac was fantastic,' she whispered. Were there stars I could see in her eyes, or only tears?

'Where *is* Zac?' I asked rather hopelessly. I could see I had lost her forever now.

'I don't really know,' she replied. 'He seemed terribly

upset after the play was over – quite broken up. I think I saw him go into the gents, but that was ages ago.'

I pushed open the door at the side of the hall and encountered empty silence. Where could he be? Then I saw him, hunched on the floor under the handbasin in his 'upset' position. He had changed into his own clothes, but his face was still streaked with 'blood' and – yes – tears.

'Why did He let them do all that?' he demanded furiously.

'Do what?' I said stupidly.

'He said Himself He could ask for Legions of Angels to scorch them all off the earth, but He didn't, He just let them do it all. Do *you* know WHY?'

Of course I did. I had learnt it all in Sunday school years before and the glib answer rolled off the tongue of the minister's son.

'He did it because He loves us.'

There was a long silence broken only by the doleful dripping of a tap.

'That's what I've been beginning to realise this last week or so,' he said at last. 'But did He just love the good people like Manda and your Dad?'

'No,' I replied miserably, 'He loves you and me just as much.'

'But when did you realise that?' he persisted.

'I've always known it I suppose,' I answered gruffly.

He sprang to his feet, his eyes flashing and his fists clenched – I really thought he was going to hit me, his whole face was flushed with anger.

'If you knew that, then why didn't you tell me,' he shouted. 'It's no fun hanging on a cross, I can tell you. It wasn't until I had to act it all just now that I realised how much it must have hurt Him. No one has ever loved *me*. Mum only cared about Kevin, and Dad only loves money.

I've lived all my life thinking no one minded if I lived or died, and all the time Jesus loved me enough to go through all that for me, and you *knew* it, but you never bothered to tell me. *Why* Davo?'

'Cool it!' I soothed. 'Stop getting so stirred up.'

'Stirred up!' he bellowed, shaking me by the collar of my shirt. 'Someone gets themselves whipped, kicked about and nailed up by the hands 'cos they love me, and you say "don't get stirred up!" I can tell you this, I'm going to spend the rest of my life telling people about Him, even if *you* can't be bothered. You just like being sorry for yourself, you do,' he spat. 'You make me sick. I'm going to ask someone to make me a Christian, right now, but I won't waste my time asking you! Manda!' he shouted as he shot out of the swing door of the gents, 'can you make people into Christians, or do I have to go to Mr Martin?'

She positively shot out of her chair, and hugged him rapturously, while her walking stick clattered to the floor behind her.

'I'd love to help you Zac,' she said, 'but you can go to Mike or David's Dad if you'd rather.'

'You'll do,' beamed Zac, and through a red haze of fury I watched them sit down next to one another — unnecessarily close I thought — as I pushed my way blindly out of the door.

Chapter Twenty

More Trouble

I don't know where I meant to go, I doubt if I thought about it really. I just wanted to put as much space between myself and that church as I possibly could. I must have wondered about Fleetbridge for a couple of hours, when I found myself in a country lane which suddenly looked familiar. Subconsciously, I had walked straight to Simon's place, and there – right in front of me was the battered old garage at the bottom of his long untidy garden.

From inside, I could hear muffled movements and subdued voices, so I tapped on the door. A sudden and rather ominous silence followed my knock.

'Who . . . Who's there?' asked an anxious voice.

'It's me, David,' I called softly. The door opened a crack and Simon's face poke out with a look of profound relief spreading over it.

'We thought you were the police,' he said in his precise, old-fashioned way.

As the Anarchists crowded round me I felt part of them at long last.

'We were just coming round to your place to get hold of you,' said Tess, hugging me for the very first time ever.

'You should just see what we've got, man,' put in Trev, 'the best drum kit I ever saw.'

Steve reverently placed a guitar in my arms like a doctor

might present a new Prince of Wales to the King of England. 'We sprayed it silver last night,' he said. 'Its own mother wouldn't know it now.'

I ran my fingers lovingly over the smooth shiny surface. 'Give it a go,' urged Monkey. 'You wait until you hear the tone.'

They had never ever been so nice to me before, and their welcome was like soothing ointment to my painful soul. Even Devil was wagging his tail.

'We've got all the gear we could ever want now,' grinned Steve. 'We've even got the possibility of a new keyboard player – we'll be in the charts in no time, but we do need you, Davo. You may be an irritating little runt sometimes, but you sound good, and your songs are magic. Will you come back to us?'

'You won't keep me away,' I laughed, as his huge hand squeezed mine in an agonising clasp, and he banged me on the back until I gasped for breath.

'We'll have a drink on it,' he said producing some champagne like a conjurer taking a rabbit from a hat.

'It's been a shame to hack all this lovely gear about,' said Simon as he screwed the last amplifier into its 'new' shabby case.

'But he's done a great job,' grinned Trev. 'Been working round the clock. Old Bill will never spot it now.'

I had never known them all in such good form as they were that day, and my heart lifted with hope as we drank to the future from a cracked collection of handleless mugs.

'What *have* you done to your hair, Davo?' laughed Tess, as she handed her mug to Steve for a refill. 'Looks as if the moths got at it.' I flushed. 'I'm skint,' I said stiffly, 'so I had to let it grow.'

'You won't be skint much longer,' cackled Steve. 'We've

got some great gigs lined up, but we must get Zac back. They all say they can get music from anywhere, but they want the drama as well. We can't make it without old Zac. What did he say when you told him we were in business again?'

'Well,' I hedged, 'he's been very busy you know with this Passion Play thing. He's going to be on ITV tonight,' I added by way of deflection. They all looked most impressed, but *oh* how bitterly I was to regret that remark.

'Give him time, he'll probably be so bored once all the excitement has died down he'll be crying for something to do.' I spoke with a lot more confidence than I really felt, and Steve must have sensed I was only stalling. Seizing me by the front of my shirt he hissed, 'Get him here Davo, or else . . .'

I looked up into Steve's sinister eyes and heard his dog snarl behind me. Cold fear was spreading through my body. You could never trust Steve, or Devil either. One minute they were your friends, and the next they might kill you.

When I finally arrived home that evening everyone was glued to the telly in the sitting room.

'Quick David,' shouted Mum, 'you're just in time.' I must say they gave the play a really good coverage. There can't have been much happening in the world that day so they were glad of something to fill the news bulletin. Zac's performance really looked most impressive, and they even included an interview with Dad about the use of drama in modern worship. But Zac was not even there to gloat over his success, he was fast asleep upstairs in bed.

I had given up in disgust. What a way to spend an Easter Bank Holiday Monday. Zac hadn't moved for nearly twenty-four hours, and I was fed up with watching him lying there like a corpse. I wanted to go round to Si's garage and experience that lovely new guitar, but I did not dare until I had talked to Zac. I had planned just what I was going to say to him. Surely I could make him see reason; but the wally just would not wake up, so I had decided in the end to take myself for a walk on the common. It was one of those magical days in early April that con you into thinking summer has arrived at last. Manda was sitting in the garden and I skidded to a halt at the sight of her on our rickety garden seat.

'Thought you'd gone to Manchester for the holidays,' I said.

'No,' she laughed, 'I've suddenly started to panic about the exams, and I thought I'd better stay here and revise.' I wanted to sit down beside her, but she was surrounded by books and files – there simply wasn't room. So there was nothing left to do, but head off in the direction of the common.

It must have been about four when I arrived home, and coming through the back garden let myself in at the kitchen door. The place looked as if a volcano had erupted. Mum must have been having a baking day. Then I remembered. The Youth Group always go on a Bank Holiday hike, finishing up at the Manse to punish their stomachs with one of Mum's buffet suppers. She had obviously got it all ready, and had gone up to have a bath. The window was open, both to let out the choking smell of burnt cake, and to let in the balmy spring air. I wondered if Manda was still out in the garden, and crossed quietly over to the window to see. She was still on the seat, but my heart sank when I saw she was not alone. Zac must have woken up at last, and she had cleared her books to make room for *him*.

I have many vices, as I have often described, and

eavesdropping just happens to be one of them. I could hear what they were saying quite clearly, and I simply sat down and listened.

At first they were just rabbiting on about how important it was to pray and read the Bible every day if you wanted to grow as a Christian. But suddenly Zac said, 'Manda, I love you.' James Bond wasn't in it. You really had to hand it to him for sheer cool nerve. I shut my eyes. I just did not want to see Manda fall into his arms. But there was such a long pause that I opened one eye and took a peep. Manda was actually laughing at him.

'You just can't stop acting can you?' she said. 'Going out with you would be like going out with a hundred different people.'

'Don't you like me then?' said Zac sounding crushed.

'Course I do,' she replied, suddenly serious. 'But I've learnt my lesson. Superstars like you and Dan don't really want to go out with a cripple, not after the first novelty's worn off. I'd always feel I was tying you down.'

'I bet you really fancy someone else,' said Zac.

There was another long pause, and then Manda said, 'I suppose you're right really. I think I've been in love with someone for months now. Someone who doesn't think very much of himself. He's always putting himself down.'

'Garry!' I thought bitterly and ground my teeth. He was always hanging round the Manse these days, and I'd been so blind I thought she was only interested in Zac.

'I always feel safe with this person,' Manda continued. 'I don't have to keep trying to live up to him.'

'Why don't you go out with him then?' asked Zac.

'There's a reason,' answered Manda bleakly. 'Let's go in now, I'm getting cold.'

Garry was all over her that evening when they all came in muddy and sweating from the hike. Dan was there too, smothering her as usual, and Zac had obviously decided not to take no for an answer; and I could have laughed watching the three of them fussing round her, if I had not been so miserable.

Zac was certainly in with the Youth Group now; in fact, he was positively the centre of it. He just could not seem to stop telling everyone how he had become a Christian, and I could not help remembering how withdrawn and cynical he had often been with the Anarchists. He had changed so dramatically it was as if he had been turned inside out. When Joan arrived with Kevin, Zac actually sat down and talked to her, promising to come round the next day and see where they lived.

'What about starting a proper church Drama Group?' said Dad suddenly, when everyone had eaten as much as politeness demanded. 'The Lord has given a lot of you a great deal of talent, and it would be super if you could keep using that to bless the whole church.'

My heart sank. I still had not had a chance to talk to Zac about the Anarchists, but I knew he would take up Dad's idea with enormous enthusiasm, and where did that leave me?

The sound of the doorbell did not interrupt the babble of excitement that met Dad's suggestion, and it was not until I saw Mum's face that I realised something was wrong.

Dad, Zac and I, responding to her urgent beckoning, followed her out into the hall.

'That police sergeant is in the study,' she whispered, and her face looked grey and pinched.

'Is my father all right?' demanded Zac, and I envied him his clear conscience. I could guess *just* why that sergeant had come.

He was not sitting in the armchair eating chocolate cake

163

this time, but stood on the hearth rug looking very grave.

'I have reason to believe that you two boys are part of a music group calling themselves the Anarchists,' he said ponderously.

'We *were*,' smiled Zac innocently.

'When were you last involved with them?' continued my favourite policeman.

'We had to disband when you arrested my father,' said Zac. 'You took all our equipment then, remember?'

'We have reason to believe you've acquired new instruments since then.' Zac looked puzzled, and I was so glad I had not told him about the break-in, at least he did not have to act this time.

'They couldn't have,' he laughed, 'they didn't have a penny between them.'

'About three hours ago, acting on information received,' continued the policeman pompously, 'we raided a garage in Pudding Lane and took into custody several members of this Anarchist group, also removed certain items of equipment which we believe were stolen from a shop in Mill Lane last Thursday night.' Simon had forgotten to remove the serial numbers – typical!

'But we haven't had any contact with that lot for weeks,' said Zac indignantly. 'I've been too busy producing this play in church. I haven't had a minute to breathe. Just because my Dad's in prison you want to pin this on me.' His voice was beginning to rise dangerously, and Dad put a hand on his shoulder.

'I'm perfectly certain you can trust this lad, Sergeant,' he said. 'He really has been far too occupied to get himself into any trouble.'

'And what about this one,' said the sergeant nastily. 'He's not *still* above suspicion is he?' He looked at me pointedly, and added, 'We've already had some trouble with *him*.'

'Look,' said Zac, trying hard to stay calm and polite. 'Whoever gave you that information, must have told you we were not involved.'

'They did tell us *you* were not involved, but we heard that this bright young lad was playing round with guitars in Pudding Lane only yesterday afternoon.' An icy silence filled the room, then Dad's voice came, as if from a great distance. 'Is that true David?' I could have lied to that sergeant easily, or to almost anyone else in the world, but Dad's eyes seemed to bore right into my soul.

'Did you help them steal the things from the music shop?'

'No.'

'Did you know they were going to do it?'

'Yes.'

'Were you using the instruments yesterday?'

'Yes.' Why was he doing the policeman's job for him, surely he should be *defending* me. Suddenly Dad's legs seemed to crumple and he sat down heavily at the desk where he prepared all his sermons, and resting his head in his hands, he looked completely defeated.

'David Martin,' boomed the police sergeant, 'I'm afraid I shall have to ask you to accompany me down to the police station to be charged with knowingly handling stolen goods.'

I shall never forget Manda's face, pressed close to the window of the police car, tears running down her cheeks. This time she was outside and I was inside. She had been innocent, but I was guilty. I cannot say which hurt me the most, the agonised expression in her eyes, or the way Dad looked as he sat in the car beside me.

I had been so sure that they would lock me up in a cell

for weeks and feed me bread and water, that it was a heady relief to be back in our own kitchen shortly after midnight. The Manse was in sombre darkness, but Mum had stayed up to warm us some milk.

Dad sank wearily into the armchair by the Aga, looking even worse than he did on a Thursday night.

'Chocolate or Ovaltine?' fussed Mum.

'No! wait,' said Dad, pushing Mum's and his own fatigue away with a little gesture of his hand. 'David, there's something your mother and I have been wanting to say to you for a long time.'

'Here it comes,' I thought. I'd been waiting since September for them to chew me up. All through those endless hours in the police station I had expected him to start on me, but what he actually said in the end, shocked me far more than if he had chucked me out of the house in just the clothes I stood up in.

'We want you to know we're sorry, David. We have failed you as parents.'

'You're . . . sorry?' I jerked, not really sure if I was hearing right.

'Yes, we've been so preoccupied with other people's troubles, it must have seemed as if we didn't care about you – we haven't been meeting your needs. We asked God what he wanted us to do about it when you first got into trouble back in the autumn. But when He told us, we were so horrified we did not dare do it.'

'What did He tell you to do?' I asked completely dazed by this time.

'Well, He showed us a verse from the Bible. It comes from 1 Timothy. It says, if a man does not know how to manage his own family, (if his children don't behave well) he cannot take care of the Church of God. So we felt that God was telling us that while you were unhappy and

166

unsettled, we must give up the leadership of this church. It's probably far too late now, but if we could live together like an ordinary family, I could try and get a secular job and have much more time to be a father. Gran's cottage in Hitchin is empty now, we could live there, and you could start all over again – do your 'A' levels away from all these bad influences. Davy, you really do mean far more to us than our Church work. God has trusted you to us as our most important priority. When you are unhappy, I have no right to stand up and preach to other people. Will you forgive us for letting you down?'

I had disgraced him before everyone who respected him, mucked up his life, and yet there he sat, solidly taking the blame. I just could not think of anything to say.

'You seemed so much better after the Anarchists disbanded,' put in Mum, 'and you started working at school again, but if we'd listened to God, then we might have saved you from all this new trouble.'

I gulped. I had waited so long to talk to them, and now my chance had come I just could not think of what to say. If I had stayed any longer I would have made a fool of myself, crying like a baby. So I dived out of the room at breakneck speed and took cover in my attic.

I did not even try to sleep. I just sat hunched on my bed. For once I was glad Zac was asleep. How could I ever explain all this to him, or Manda for that matter. They adored my Mum and Dad. How could I tell them they were leaving this house and the church just because of me? What would Zac and Manda do? Where would they live? I had always liked John, but he was still not very stable. Suppose he went back on to heroin without the support Mum and Dad gave him? Pam was a pain, but this was her home now, and what sort of a mess would Joan be in without our house to escape to? Even smelly old George would go hungry and cold. My selfishness was going to affect all these people, not to mention the hundreds who relied on Dad at church.

I felt like a rotten, dirty, little slug, and that's not a nice way to feel. I just could not let that happen, and anyway, the prospect of living in a tiny cottage with Mum and Dad having nothing else to do but watch me work for 'A' levels, was not a stimulating prospect. I must see Dad in the morning, talk everything out with him; stop him making this ghastly mistake.

Chapter Twenty-One

A Terrifying Climax

It must have been Zac tiptoeing out of our bedroom that finally woke me next day. I groped for my watch and found to my horror it was well after midday. There was something terribly important I had to do. I leapt out of bed trying desperately to remember what it was. I had to see Dad, that was it. Dad! Yes I had to talk to Dad. But as I hurtled downstairs two at a time, I sensed the house was abnormally quiet. Manda was sitting at the kitchen table surrounded once again by her school books, while Zac fondled a mug of coffee with his feet on the table. They both shot up as I burst into the room, question marks all over their faces.

'They think Tess and I will go on probation,' I said to put them out of their misery, 'but they kept the others locked up overnight. They'll be coming up before the magistrate today.'

'What about Michelle?' asked Zac.

'She seems to have kept her nose clean,' I replied, 'but Big Jim's girlfriend is in it up to her neck.'

'But where's Dad?' I asked urgently.

'They've gone to London,' replied Manda. 'Told me to tell you they'd gone to see someone called Gerald Meekin.'

'Oh no!' I gasped. We don't have Bishops in our Church, but Gerald Meekin was our equivalent of one.

Dad must really have meant what he said and he had gone to resign from the Church. I looked hopelessly at Manda and Zac, and then round this kitchen where so many people felt safe and loved. I even looked at the ceiling, and I would not have been surprised if it had suddenly caved in and covered us with rubble.

'Who on earth is Gerald Meekin?' asked Zac. I did not want to tell him, and for once I was glad of the sound of the doorbell; it gave me an excuse to get away from their questions. But when I opened the door no one was there, yet I had a horrid feeling someone was watching me. Down on the mat at my feet lay a piece of grubby paper, and I bent to pick it up. Someone *was* out there hiding in the garden. I sensed a definite impression of danger.

'What *is* up?' demanded Zac, tweeking the paper out of my hand and reading it aloud to Manda.

> 'David
> Come at once to Si's garage.
> Bring Zac with you, OR ELSE . . .'

'That's Steve's scrawl,' said Zac, 'I'd know it anywhere. They must have got bail. Poor twits, they'll all be at Si's scared out of their minds. We'd better go round there right now, they'll need all the support they can get.'

'Steve's never been scared of anything in his life,' I protested.

'Sometimes you're blind as a stone, Davo,' said Zac witheringly. 'Didn't you know that Steve's father's been knocking him round since he was a baby? I've been thinking about them all lots just lately. They're all miserable and uptight about something. They need Jesus to change their lives too, just like I did. I'm going round there to tell them about Him.'

170

'They wouldn't want to know!' I protested. 'They like living their own lives.'

'No they don't,' said Zac. 'They've all got such horrible lives that being part of the group was their only escape. Now they haven't even got that. You ought to have told us all right from the start that there was something more to living.'

'I value my skin,' I shuddered.

'Well Jesus didn't value His, and when it came to doing something for *you* did He?'

'You've only been a Christian a few days,' I said crossly, 'so stop preaching, or you'll get yourself hurt.'

I was in a complete quandary. I was terrified of what Steve might do to me if I did not get Zac round to Simon's place, and yet I felt instinctively that he would be in great danger if he went. I looked imploringly at Manda for support.

'You must be careful of Steve,' she said cautiously. 'He's a Satanist.'

'All the more reason why he needs Jesus,' said Zac.

'Let me come with you,' said Manda uneasily.

'It's right across the common in Pudding Lane,' I said firmly. 'You'd never walk that far.'

'You could push me in the wheelchair.' But I shook my head firmly. I would give anything I possessed to keep her from any possible harm.

'You stay here and pray for us,' said Zac, as he ran out of the door. But I detected a mulish look of determination on her face that only added to my worries.

We had walked right into a trap. I knew it the moment the little side door of the garage shut behind us, and Steve had locked it, slowly putting the key into his pocket. The girls were not there, but when I saw the expressions on the faces of the other five Anarchists, I turned cold and clammy with fear. There was no escape. Simon's cupboards and workbench were piled up against the double garage doors and the window was too small even for a runt like me to dive through.

'Last time we saw you, Zaccy Boy, you was on TV nailed up on a cross. Nice to see you've recovered.'

'We're not too pleased with you Zac,' snarled Trev. 'Gone off and formed your own group of little church prigs have you? We're not good enough for you now?'

'It's not like that,' protested Zac. 'Davo's Dad's been very good to me, and I wanted to help him out. But I did want to tell you that doing that Passion Play really has changed my life. I've realised Jesus Christ is a real person, and He's still alive. He gives you something to live for.'

'Jesus Christ!' exploded Monkey. 'It's always Jesus Christ!'

'So that's why you shopped us was it?' spat Steve. 'Turned so pure your conscience pricked you, so you squealed all the way to the pig sty?'

'I never grassed on you,' protested Zac. 'I didn't even know you'd done that job until the police came on Monday night, and *they* believed me.'

'But is *has* to be you,' screamed Monkey. 'Michelle saw you leaving the pig sty on Monday afternoon.'

'She couldn't have,' said Zac. 'I never went out of the house on Monday.'

'Liar!' rasped Steve, and Devil showed his wicked teeth. 'Coming here with your *holy holy holy* talk and all the while you knew you'd cut our throats. So you want to be like Jesus Christ! I wonder if you *really do*. Got any long nails Si?'

Simon dug them out of a drawer and handed them to Steve with a hammer. Really I don't think he believed

Steve would use them any more than I did. We thought he was just messing about – trying to give Zac a fright. But suddenly we were caught up in the middle of a nightmare, as Steve, Jim and Trev lunged at Zac, pinning him against the wooden wall of the garage. I caught sight of Jim's face and realised that Zac, his idol, had fallen finally from the pedestal, and Jim would never forgive him for spoiling the first great plan of his life. He is almost as big as Steve, and physically even stronger. He stood on Zac's feet and pressed his massive shoulder into his chest.

'Don't be stupid,' gasped Zac. 'At least give me a chance to prove I didn't shop you.' But it was useless, something evil had taken possession of Steve, and nothing could stop him now. He forced his grubby handkerchief into Zac's mouth and gagged him with a dirty bit of cheesecloth that lay on Si's workbench. 'Pull his arm out straight, Trev,' he ordered.

I shall never forget the horrible sound of that hammer. Si's face went a sickly green and he turned hastily away. If I could have seen myself, I think I would have been the same colour. I never have been able to stand the sight of blood, but I knew I ought to do something, yet I was terrified of Steve, and even more afraid of his dog. Heroes on TV would have dealt with this situation effortlessly, but I was no hero, and I felt that ghastly dirty slug feeling creeping over me again.

'Now for the other hand,' said Steve triumphantly, and I had to shut my eyes.

'How does that feel now Jesus Christ?' mocked Steve stepping back to survey Zac spreadeagled against the wall, his eyes dark with agony – he was not acting this time. 'Now we'll teach you what we think of narks.' He threw the hammer contemptuously at Si, and began to punch Zac's face with his huge fists as if he intended to fracture his skull.

'Put the brake on Steve,' said Trev nervously. 'He's bound to squeal about this too, and we'll go down for GBH.'

'It would be a pleasure to go down for murder,' cackled Steve. 'This poser thought he owned me with all his money. Come on Jim you can have a go.'

They had been Zac's friends for years – they had lived off him like leeches – how could they turn on him like this?

'Stop them Monkey!' I implored. 'Crucifying Jesus Christ never did you Jews much good. If you kill Zac it would ruin all your lives.' I could see Monkey understood me, and he said, 'You've given him enough now, Steve, let's get out of here.'

'You're not going anywhere,' said Steve, patting the pocket of his jeans.

'Give me that key,' demanded Monkey, springing at Steve like a wild cat. But Devil leapt into action and his teeth closed viciously on Monkey's skinny arm.

'Get him off,' screamed Monkey, but Steve only laughed. 'Guard him Devil,' he ordered, and turned back to punish Zac with renewed venom.

They were going to kill Zac. Something had to be done quickly. I looked wildly round the garage. Simon had disappeared under a table, Monkey lay on the floor with Devil standing over him, while Trev had backed into a corner pulverised with fear.

'Do something God!' I prayed urgently inside my head. 'Zac only came here for your benefit, don't let him down now.' But no earthquake shook the garage and no angel appeared and I had the nasty feeling that God wanted me to do something about it myself.

Steve was punching Zac in the ribs by this time, in a way that must have made breathing with that gag in his mouth very difficult indeed, and suddenly sheer rage lent me all the courage I needed. I hate rugger even more than I loathe all other forms of sport, but for my first tackle ever I did quite well, catching Steve round the top of his jeans, and bringing his heavy body crashing on to the concrete floor. Devil had been told to guard Monkey, so thank God he never moved, but Steve wrenched himself out of my grasp and his great fist descended on my nose. I knew it was broken yet again. I was getting pretty used to the sensation by that time. I don't know how many times he hit me, but I didn't care, because I had held the door key in my hand.

'If you do that again, Davo,' he said contemptuously, 'I'll set Devil onto you.' It was as he stood up that I saw the face at the window. Could it possibly be Dan, and was that Garry behind him? I never thought I'd be so glad to see those two. I remembered the mutinous look on Manda's face. She must have rounded them up. But how many more of the Youth Group had she got out there, and how was I going to let them in? Between me and the door stood Devil.

''ere, Steve, don't hit him again, he's gone all limp.' Jim's voice sounded frightened. Zac had slumped forward, his legs crumpled and all his weight was suspended on those two cruel nails.

'He's dead man!' croaked Trev, sidling out of the shadows. Simon emerged from under his table, peering nervously through his steamy glasses, and Steve said, 'You'd better have a look at him, Monkey, you're always saying you want to be a doctor. Devil, leave him!'

Monkey struggled uncertainly to his feet. Blood was seeping through the gashes in his shirt, but when he looked at Zac he did not seem to notice it. They were all clustered round Zac now, here was my chance. I leapt for the door and rammed the key into the lock, but even as I pushed open the door, I panicked. Devil was behind me and he was dangerous. If the others tried to come in now, someone else might well be killed, so I turned round to confront him myself. I had seen Manda out there in Si's garden, and no way was that savage dog going to get near her.

There was another David once who killed a lion with his bare hands. I'm not sure if that's what I intended to do, but I cannot recall the animal biting my face. All I remember is my hands closing round his studded collar, as I forced his head away with all my strength. It was Dan who leapt in through the door whipping off his jacket to cover Devil's head. Then he picked the animal up bodily and threw him into the dirty little outside loo, and banged the door shut behind him. Garry, Dominic, John and Peter had to jump over my sprawled body to get into the garage, but I did manage to wriggle out of the way before Pam hurtled Manda through the door like Queen Boadicea in her wheelchair.

Monkey, Simon and Trev were so relieved to see them they gave up without a fight. Jim always was a coward, but it was obvious that Steve was going to fight to the death. Dan took him on, while the others were busy rounding up the rest of the Anarchists. But even he was no match for Steve, who had him on the ground in no time. I shall never ever forget the extraordinary sight of Manda leaning out of her wheelchair and cracking Steve on the head with her walking stick.

In no time they were all huddled in a heap with their hands and legs tied securely with the laces from HiTec boots, and Pam and Manda's tights.

'David you're hurt!' Manda's face was nothing but a blur as she bent over me.

'Don't worry about me,' I gasped. 'Zac's dead!'

John found some pliers on Si's workbench, and carefully

he and Garry pulled out the nails, while Dan laid Zac's rag-doll body down on the floor, supporting his battered head on Pam's fluffy cardigan. Dominic was sick all over the floor.

'I never can remember where you have to feel for a pulse,' muttered Dan as he bent over Zac. 'I just can't seem to feel one anywhere.'

'You've killed him!' shouted Manda, her face flushed with fury as she glared at the pile of Anarchists. 'We need the police.'

'No . . . police.' Everybody jumped.

'Who said that?' demanded Dan.

'No . . . police.' The disembodied voice came again.

'We thought you were dead,' I sobbed. Because I had been lying on the floor, I had been the first to realise it was Zac speaking.

Relief washed over us, only to be replaced by further concern. Zac was losing a lot of blood and he was obviously having a job to breathe.

'We must get an ambulance,' said Dan firmly.

'No ambulance,' muttered Zac. 'Too many questions. Must prove I'm not a nark.'

'What's he on about?' said Dan appealing to me.

'They think he told the police about the break-in they did last week,' I explained. 'He came round here to tell them about Jesus, so I suppose he thinks they won't ever listen to him if he gets them into more trouble.'

'But he's got to have medical help quickly,' protested Dan, as Zac's eyes closed and he seemed to drift off into another faint.

'I know!' exclaimed Manda. 'My Uncle Mike lives just over the common. If one of you pushed me in the chair, we could fetch him in less than five minutes.'

'No,' moaned Zac weakly, but Manda and Dan were off and away out of the door.

An ominous silence settled over the garage, only Devil's outraged yelps could be heard from the loo outside. But suddenly feet were pounding up the lane towards us, and through the door ran Doctor Davidson, followed by my father.

Chapter Twenty-Two

God's Victory

Dad had come straight from London to hand in his resignation to the Doctor, who was also the Church Secretary, and they had been sitting in his lounge when Dan had practically catapulted Manda in through the french windows. Manda must have explained the situation to them as they all ran back – she was the only person who would have had enough breath! All the same, I think they were both completely unprepared for the shock of seeing Zac.

'What sort of fiend did this to him?' murmured Dr Davidson as he opened his medical bag and went into action.

Dad bent over me, and said, 'Manda told us you had been very brave, David. I'm proud of you.'

Dad proud of a slug like me! I would have been completely happy if my face hadn't hurt so much.

'We'll have to get him to hospital,' said Dr Davidson straightening his back. 'He's not in very good shape, and I'm afraid there'll be some internal injuries. Can someone get the police?'

'No!' Zac's eyes stared compellingly up at the Doctor.

'You mean you really want to let this horrible bunch get away with it?' exclaimed the Doctor looking at the Anarchists in disgust.

'Please Dad,' I whispered. Dad got up and stood looking

down at Zac. 'Father, forgive them, they know not what they do,' he murmured. 'I think we must do what he wants, Mike.'

'But what sort of a story am I going to tell the hospital?' protested the Doctor.

'If Zac keeps quiet and refuses to press charges, there's nothing the police can do,' replied Dad; and looking round at the rest of us, he added, 'I'm trusting all of you to keep this secret, if that's what Zac really wants.'

While the Doctor went to ring for an ambulance, most ministers would not have been able to resist preaching a sermon to a captive audience. But as my Dad untied the Anarchists, all he said to them as they ran for the door was 'God bless you.'

At the hospital, Zac had VIP treatment and was trundled away on a trolley. I was told to wait for a nurse to come and pack my nose, after the Doctor had stitched up the dog bite on my cheek. 'Then you will have a tetanus injection,' they told me, as if they were saving their very best as a treat for good behaviour. They shoved me in behind those dreaded curtains, and I hoped they would not pump out my stomach by mistake.

In the distance, I could hear Dad talking to the police.

'If the lad is only sixteen, he is hardly in a position *not* to press charges,' said a familiar official voice.

'But I am his guardian,' Dad replied, 'and I do not want to make any complaint on his behalf, or on that of my own son.' I grinned in spite of my painful face. What a crazy man my father was, but how like the Jesus he served.

When his face peeped round the curtains, I asked him, 'What did Gerald Meekin say?'

'He's in America,' said Dad, 'so I want all that way for nothing.'

'But you talked to Doctor Davidson?'

'I'm afraid I haven't got round to it yet,' he replied apologetically. 'We got a bit interrupted.'

'Good,' I said shyly. 'Dad don't do it. I'd hate to live in Hitchin, and I don't ever want to leave the Manse or any of the lame dogs or deep problems.'

'But David . . .'

'Dad I'm sorry. I've messed everything up. Can't we start again?'

'The best thing about God is that you always can,' beamed Dad.

'I don't really think I ever knew God for myself,' I said quietly. 'I've always relied on you and Mum. I've been lying here thinking I'd like to have God right inside me like the rest of you.'

Dad blew his nose loudly, but all he said was, 'Manda *will* be pleased.'

'What's it got to do with her?' I asked puzzled.

'She's been in love with you for months, you silly old chump, but she wouldn't go out with someone who wasn't a real Christian.'

The Doctor changed his mind, and decided to keep me in hospital for forty-eight hours. He said I was suffering from shock, but I did not like to tell him it was not the dog bite or the broken nose that caused my condition.

They put me in a bed next to Zac, but he was not exactly good company; in fact he was fast asleep – just for a change. He did not really wake up until the following evening when Sister opened the swing doors for the visitors to come in. It was Manda who was the first to hobble into the ward. She waved to Zac, but it was my bed she sat down beside.

I fumbled for her hand, and felt as if my temperature must have rocketed to 106°.

'I would really rather like to kiss you,' she whispered,

'but your face is so plastered up I just can't see a space.'

'Manda I . . . Manda will you . . . ?' I had practised this speech all day. 'Would you . . . ?' It was the story of my life. Just at that crucial moment a huge kerfuffle began at the far end of the ward.

'Only two visitors per patient,' declared Sister, but the Anarchists took no notice of her whatever, and surged down between the rows of beds, their DMs clumping on the polished floor. Monkey had his arm in a sling, and they all looked thoroughly sheepish.

'We . . . we came to see how you were,' began Steve as they deposited what seemed like two tons of chocolate and sweets on to Zac's bed.

'It was . . . it was Michelle who ratted,' said Monkey awkwardly. 'She got fed up with Steve chasing Tess, so she decided to spite us all.'

'Really, I must ask you to leave,' fussed Sister, and shooed them away down the ward like farmyard chickens. But Monkey looked back at Zac over his shoulder and said, 'If this Jesus Christ can change anyone as much as He's changed you, maybe he *is* our Messiah after all.'

Epilogue

It's all because of the daffodils. There's a great bunch of them stuck in a vase here on the table, and they keep peering at me over the mountain of history books I'm supposed to be marking. But I can never look a daffodil in the face without remembering that Easter twelve years ago. So many memories have been surging round in my mind, those essays will never be ready to hand back tomorrow at school.

It's lovely living here in Gran's little cottage in Hitchin, but the poor old place creaks a bit trying to hold all my books. No, I'm not a famous minister, people *don't* travel the world to hear me preach, or ask my advice. I'm just an ordinary history teacher, but I'm a round peg in a round hole and I'm happy.

And Zac? I have to laugh when I think about him. He's become all that I dreamed I'd be. The church where he is the minister is now so crowded they're having to build a new one! Kevin died of pneumonia two years ago, and Zac was with him in the hospital right to the end. You could not exactly describe Zac and his mother as 'close' because they will never really 'click' as people; all the same they have worked very hard on their relationship. But it was Kevin Zac really loved.

It would be nice to be able to say that all the Anarchists became Christians sitting on Zac's hospital bed. But it always amazes me that even when people *know* how much Jesus loves them and wants to help them in their problems, they can still turn away and reject Him.

It was not much fun being on probation, but it was far worse for the others who got six months Youth Custody for their visit to Mill Lane. That finished Simon's hopes of Oxbridge, but he has done very well indeed working in computer design.

I think Steve's been in and out of prison several times, but he and Tess still managed to produce five children before she was twenty-two. I'd *like* to be able to say Devil died of rabies, but I believe he lived on to a ripe old age.

Michelle had been taking drugs since she was thirteen. 'Speed' was the only thing that gave her the pace during that time with the group, but when Tess and Steve finally got together, she drifted on to heroin. I met her in Fleetbridge the day I got my 'A' level results, shuffling through the High Street like a shaky old woman. She couldn't even remember my name. I've never seen her since.

We lost touch with Trev completely, but the other day I was sure I saw him in Top of the Pops on telly, drumming with a group called Black Ash. I couldn't be sure, but surely no one else has eight arms – he really did deserve to get to the top.

There's a postcard on the mantelpiece. It's been there for two years, but we haven't the heart to take it down. There's a picture of Lake Galilee on it. When Monkey finished his Youth Custody, the whole family moved to Israel and that postcard is all the news we've had in eleven years. It says, 'Sorry, no time to write – too busy telling people out here about their Messiah. Give Zac my love and thank him for everything.' He finished with a pin man standing on its head and signs himself Dr

'Monkey'. So maybe he did make it in medicine after all.

There's a lovely smell coming from the kitchen. I've put on so much weight since I got married. At least my wife does not have to compete with her mother-in-law (who is still burning cakes in Fleetbridge).

We'll probably have supper in here by the fire – I still come over dizzy when I think of a girl like Manda actually marrying someone like me! Of course, we haven't lived happily ever after, perhaps no one ever does. We had planned at least four children, so when the doctors told us that Manda should never have a baby because of the damage to her back and legs, it was a tragic blow; and even now I sometimes wake in the night and find her crying. But she never has time in the day to grieve, not with her job and the stream of people who come to see her. It's almost as bad as living with Mum and Dad again. But now I find I like the people myself, and I never call them the 'Deep Problems' because I'm hurting with them. Our lives are never boring.

Miss Carmichael once told me that I would grow up when I dared to be myself. Well I'm not the superstar I imagined I'd be. Perhaps growing up meant accepting that I never will be. I can't say I'm any happier now when I look in the mirror. My face is badly scarred, my nose is still a mess, and the craters the spots left behind remind me of the surface of the moon. But I wouldn't change places with anyone else on this earth, because I know it's *me* Manda loves, and the *real* me that God loves, and what more does any man want, anyway?

THE END

If you wish to receive *regular information* about *new books,* please send your name and address to:

London Bible Warehouse
PO Box 123
Basingstoke
Hants RG23 7NL

Name _____

Address _____

_____

_____

_____

I am especially interested in:
- [ ] Biographies
- [ ] Fiction
- [ ] Christian living
- [ ] Issue related books
- [ ] Academic books
- [ ] Bible study aids
- [ ] Children's books
- [ ] Music
- [ ] Other subjects

P.S. If you have ideas for new Christian Books or other products, please write to us too!

The Long Summer   *Eleanor Watkins*

A sizzling hot summer holiday adventure for James, Katie and Paul. There has not been as much as a cloud in the sky for weeks, just sun and more sun. The stream has dried up and the earth is cracked and hard. On a farm camping holiday, a surprise discovery saves the animals and wildlife which are dying of thirst, but trapped by a raging hill fire themselves, the children remember the farmer telling them about the *Living Water*.

£1.60

The Ponies of Swallowdale Farm   *Sue Garnett*

Cassie loves horses more than anything else. Helping at Mrs. Cole's stables in return for free rides, she is heartbroken at her family's news that they are to move to the Lake District.

As they near their new rectory home, the beautiful mountain scenery turns Cassie's despair into delight. But it is short lived and all her hopes of ever riding again are dashed when she meets the stuck-up girl whose father owns the trekking stables nearby.

Why does she hate Cassie so much? Why, with all those horses, is she so miserable? Cassie *must* win her friendship, but how?

£1.75

All Alone (Except for my dog Friday) *Claire Blatchford*

'Dear Girl, go home'. Margaret found the note on her desk. Who had written it? Was it one of her friends she had had before she lost her hearing? They all seemed to ignore her now. In fact, Margaret was sure no-one understood what it was like to be deaf. Not her parents, nor even her brother, Frank. No one – except a lovable stray sheep-dog called Friday.

But the comfort he brings to Margaret is spoiled by her constant fears that his owners will come and claim him, and leave her – once again – all alone.

£1.60

The Music Plays Past Midnight *Marilyn Cram Donahue*

Syl both looked and felt a nobody. Wherever she went, if people weren't being rude or making fun at her, they just put up with her and hoped she'd go away. Caro felt sorry for her in a way, but drew the line at becoming friends. She could never live *that* down among the rest of the crowd. Yet Syl seemed so unhappy, she couldn't turn her back on her, and together, despite all the odds, they discover the best of friendships.

£1.60

The Fire Brand
Jennifer Rees

Jake, who had lived all his life in and out of a children's home, was on his way to yet another foster home. He had hated them all so far and was all ready to behave in his usual wild, rebellious way which had earned him his nickname – The Fire Brand.

But the Jarvis family turn out to be different from all the others, and Jake is surprised to find himself changing too.

In *The Fire Brand*, discover the reason for Jake's happy surprise.

95p

The Great Darkness
Wendy Green

What happens when a teenage boy from a primitive culture meets a girl from the computer age, after the world has been taken over by a robot government?

Together, Um and the girl defy the authority of 'the Box' and discover a new meaning to their lives.

£1.25